When Matt Killian, a LAPD cop-turned-private-eye, is approached one rainy day in Hollywood to take on a missing person case, he initially wants to say "no" when the potential client tells him he chose Killian because he's gay. Killian changes his mind, however, when he learns the man is distraught because his son, Dane Marks—AKA notorious gay porn director, Danny Dark—is missing. Matt is further surprised to learn that Dane has already tried to take his own life, twice, and has now disappeared, possibly to escape interference in his third attempt.

It's a race against time as Killian tracks down Danny Dark and attempts to short-circuit the man's desire for self-destruction. Plunged headlong into the sometimes-amusing, sometimes-terrifying world of gay porn, Killian is mistaken for a go-go dancer and performs in a live show to get close to Dane.

This book has been previously published.

Love For Sale
Copyright © 2019 A.J. Llewellyn
ISBN: 978-1-4874-2461-9
Cover art by Martine Jardin

Published by eXtasy Books Inc or
Devine Destinies, an imprint of eXtasy Books Inc

Look for us online at:
www.eXtasybooks.com or www.devinedestinies.com

# Love For Sale

## By

## A.J. Llewellyn

# DEDICATION

*To David Byrne and The Talking Heads whose fantastic song inspired this title. Thank you for making music that helps me write!*

# CHAPTER ONE

It started out a weird morning that Saturday. The weather was rough. Storms had pounded the west coast for over a week and the early morning radio report carried the unwelcome news that the worst barrage of a freak, three storm pile-up was coming this weekend.

I stood at the sliding glass balcony doors of my Santa Monica apartment, watching the rain fill the small cement enclosure. Up to three inches now. My cat, Ronin, stood beside me, staring out at the carnage being done to his favorite place to snooze. Water had been seeping in through the edges of the frame into the apartment. I'd hauled in all the outdoor plants a couple of days ago and my favorite chair.

I'd banked up towels, blankets, whatever I could against the glass and was now out of anything extra to add to the pile. I contemplated wadding bed sheets against the soaked towels that were beginning to smell musty. The rain came down so hard the small drains in the corners of the balcony couldn't cope with the deluge. It had been like this for two days. A small break in the inclement weather meant the water could drip out, slowly. But now it hadn't stopped for two hours.

*Yeah, I just had to move me to Santa Monica.*

I stared out at the grey clouds, the sky and the horizon merging into one another. Living on Speedway seemed such a great idea three weeks ago when my brother had wanted to up and move to New York, offering me his longtime home as a sublease.

It seemed like a gift from Heaven. Now it felt like punishment.

The beach communities up and down the coast were suffering the worst of the onslaught. I'd heard on the news that the valley was enjoying dry, pleasant and sunny weather. *Spiffing*. And I'd been cracking my neck to move from there . . .

I sipped the first and what I expected to be my only cup of coffee of the day. I was down to twelve bucks in my bank account. I'd just paid down my credit card and didn't much feel like hiking it back up again.

Even for staples like coffee.

"Meow," Ronin said.

"Back at you, bitch." I smiled down at my geriatric cat, who didn't take offense. He loved me. He knew, somehow, that his name meant *Samurai without a master* in Japanese. He knew I didn't consider myself his superior. I saw him as a companion. He rubbed his head against my ankle and padded off, looking for something else to do.

The badly neutered, completely declawed, totally deranged, ancient Maine Coon was a sweet cat who had a bad habit of spraying if I stayed away from home too long. But he was also psycho. He liked having me around since I was the guy who fed him primo canned food *and* fresh chicken, but he did not like me kipping on *his* bed. His first week living with me, he'd peed on it when I tried to get under the covers.

I'd managed to get him out of the peeing-on-the-bed-habit. Every other place was to him, fair game. I watched him squat in one of the potted plants.

*Yeah, I just had to rescue me a cat at a mobile adoption unit on the boardwalk.*

Those manipulative ASPCA workers knew a sucker when they saw one. So had Ronin, who was so spectacular-looking they'd given him the name Hollywood. He was a heartbreaker with his long, golden coat and big sad eyes. He'd been turned in by his owners, who'd claimed he was a stray. The shelter volunteers told me he'd been estimated by their vet to be ten years old.

They casually mentioned he probably wouldn't last long at the shelter.

"Older cats and big dogs are the first to be euthanized," they told me.

I took pity on the poor thing. Under his fur as I held him, I could feel mats the size of small mice. And I could feel his bones.

*Starved.* They guesstimated he was five or six pounds underweight.

He also had a broken fang and broken tailbone.

To me he looked like a boxer who'd been through a crushing twelve-round bout and hadn't picked up the will to swallow down a meal yet.

I'd taken him to a nearby vet with the coupon the shelter gave me. Dr. Mood had broken the news that my new kitty was probably closer to thirteen and had bad teeth all around. "His kinky tail probably happened at birth."

Ronin bit the vet's hand. "And, he has an attitude problem."

*I* have an attitude problem, so I figured Ronin and I were meant to be.

The masterless samurai Ronin began pawing at the sofa. I sighed. This was usually what he did before he started spraying. The first time I saw him doing it I had no idea what was going on. He simply backed up against the wall, his tail started to shake, and he'd moved away again revealing a running stream of pee.

I yelled at him, and he stopped pawing. I shook my head at him. He didn't understand that running around after him, cleaning up his pee, using the variety of substances I had to rub and spray onto the surfaces he contaminated was an expensive proposition.

All he understood was that *I* was the samurai, he was the master, and I wasn't making the rain stop. Or something. Ronin could get easily pissed about . . . anything.

Lately, I could walk in and smell the pee in the apartment but couldn't find the places he'd hosed. I'd invested in a black light from Petco that I could only use at night. It illuminated the cat pee and, to my horror, my new home looked like a crime scene.

Ronin didn't understand that my nerves were just about shattered. I'd come off a difficult case and still hadn't been paid the final installment. Each day brought a fresh wave of disappointment when the check didn't arrive. As for new cases, Ronin didn't seem to realize we lived in LA, the only place in the world I knew of where people begged off doing anything because of rain.

That included booking private investigators for work. It had been two weeks since my last job, and I was beginning to wonder if I should give up my small office on the northwest corner of Wilshire Boulevard and 23rd Street.

I stared into the bottom of my cup. Could I really live on one cup of coffee for a day?

From the corner of my eye, I caught Ronin's tail beginning to shake.

"Ronin!"

He'd backed up against the front door and knew he was in trouble but couldn't stop in midstream. I watched him slink away, the familiar film of yellow streaking down the door. I quickly cleaned, sprayed, dried and kept up a stream of verbal abuse that would have shamed a sailor.

And then my phone rang.

A man's voice. "Matt Killian?"

"Yes," I said. I was a little surprised. The only people who had my landline number were my brother, his landlord and the landlord from my office building.

"It's Jack Banning."

Ah. My landlord from the office building.

"There's someone in your office," he said. "I let the guy in, but I hear him opening drawers and stuff. Probably you wanna come check."

"What? You just let a stranger in?"

"He said he was your partner."

"My *what*? I don't have a partner. You know that."

A long pause. "Sorry, Matt." I could tell Jack had been drinking. I sighed. His wife had just left him for the guy who used to rent my office space. Jack had taken it badly.

"I'll be right there." I had no idea what the hell was going on but whatever it was sure beat the heck out of playing slave to the pee master.

Ronin watched me with a mulish expression as I grabbed my rain slicker, keys, wallet and cell phone and unlocked the front door. He sat on the sofa, his head tilted at an odd angle. He'd never tried to run out the door. Not once. He liked it in my apartment. From everything I'd read, the peeing was a territorial thing.

"I won't be long," I told the cat. He just looked at me. I swear to God I could read his damned thoughts.

*Liar.*

I walked to 23rd, not because it was close. It was twenty-three blocks, but I needed the exercise. It was nice to get out, even in the pouring rain. At least that was my plan until I crossed the lights at third and found myself ankle-deep in water. The streets were flooded. I went back home, fished my car out of the subterranean garage where I noticed to my dismay the water building up to the bumper bar. I made it to the office seventeen minutes later.

My shoes squelched, and my car was miserable. The lights flickered on and off on the dash as I parked inside the garage. It was bone dry. Of course it was. I pondered leaving the car there when I was done as I climbed the stairs to the second floor.

The lights were on in my office, and I could see the shadow of a head illuminated in the frosted glass. I felt like an old-style gumshoe with the words Matt Killian Investigations stenciled on it.

It was a man, judging by what I heard. He was talking. On his cell phone or my landline?

"Nope . . . not here yet. Sandy, I'll call you as soon he gets here."

I turned the handle and opened the office door. The man in the guest chair turned and looked at me. I noticed three things in the blink of an eye. Firstly, my office had been tossed. Secondly, the man was older. Around sixty. Thirdly, he looked distraught.

"Did you do this?" I asked as I walked inside and closed the door.

The man looked offended. "Certainly not. It was like this when I got here. Actually, I may have seen the perpetrator. Somebody was leaving as I walked in for my appointment."

I gaped at him. What was more shocking? The fact that he'd seen somebody coming out of here or that he thought we had an appointment?

Desperate for business, I didn't want to sound like a complete dickhead, so I asked, "What did he look like?"

The man shrugged. He looked elegant. I definitely put him in his sixties, and I could see he was deeply anguished.

"I don't know. Dark haired." He paused, screwing up his eyes as if he were trying to banish the memory. "He had a weird hair cut. A sort of flat Mohawk. The sides and back of his head were bald, but the top had hair. Yeah. Like I said, a flat Mohawk. It wasn't an attractive look."

"Okay," I said. I had no idea who the guy might have been. I moved to my chair on the other side of the desk. I wanted to offer the man sitting opposite me some coffee. Or tea. However, the coffee carafe, my swanky new Keurig system was gone. As was the electric kettle I used for coffee. Dang. My awards, license, the two photos I kept on my desk and, for the life of me, how anyone could steal my collection of *Spiderman* comics, which should have been sacred, but shit. They were gone too.

I sat in my chair. *I* was the one in deep anguish now.

"It looked like he'd stuck a road-killed skunk on his head if you want to know," the man went on.

*No, I don't.* I took inventory of all my stuff that was missing. Whoever had been in here had left me the desk and two chairs. And a pen. That was thoughtful of him.

"He was wearing ugly shorts. He's got a lot of tattoos, and he smelled like —" The man stopped speaking.

"Like what?" I looked up at him, then glanced back at the desk. I'd just noticed three pretty good fingerprints on my desk.

"Glue. I know it sounds weird. But he smelled like glue."

I stared at him. Maybe the guy was a glue sniffer. Whip-Its were the hot new drug for broke people. Inhaling the gas from cans of whipped cream or the fumes from glue were the affordable drugs of choice for idiots who didn't know better.

My filing cabinets were still in the office, but when I got up to look at them, I could see somebody had tried to force them open. I kept my rain slicker on since we weren't going to be long and unlocked the first cabinet. My crime scene kit was in there from my recent history with the Los Angeles Metro Police Department. I'd been forced to quit after being shot in the line of duty. Some people got gold watches and parachutes. I got a hip injury that forced me out of my passion for motorbike duty and rendered me useless, according to my superiors, by being stuck behind a desk.

And here I was. I lifted out the kit, dusted the prints. It took me a moment to realize the man had stopped talking. I dusted the cabinets and the back of my chair. I was pissed that somebody had infiltrated my privacy. And for what? My gaze swiveled to the empty wicker box that had, up until yesterday, contained my Spidey collection. None were valuable, though I tried to delude myself that they were.

I sighed. My fax machine and scanner combo was still there. I picked up my cell phone and called my former lover, Stu Gressing, now working as a detective in the notorious South West Division's vice unit.

"Got a favor," I said as the man in the seat opposite stared at me.

"Don't you always?" Stu sighed. He was so damned theatrical. "Okay, hit me."

"I've had a break-in."

"Don't you always?"

He had me there. This wasn't the first one. But this time the shit got personal with my missing Keurig and the Spidey comics.

"What do you need from me?" he asked finally.

"Got some prints. Can I send 'em to you?"

"Sure. It'll take a bit o' time. We got a huge vice thing goin' on. It might be raining, but the hookers aren't taking a holiday. They've set up shop in the school playground over on Adams."

*Nice.* "Sorry to hear it."

Hookers, vice, and Adams. Business as usual for Stu.

"Thanks," he said. He ended the call. I knew it wouldn't take long. Stu and I were still close. We'd loved each other once until he decided he didn't want me anymore . . . well, actually, he'd decided he didn't want to be *gay* anymore. Still, he looked out for me, and I knew he'd get back to me sooner rather than later.

I scanned the prints and emailed them to Stu.

"The reason I called you was because you're gay."

I turned from the workbench and stared at the man in the chair. For a moment I'd forgotten he was even there.

"What's that supposed to mean?" Before he could respond, my cell phone beeped. I stared at it. A 310 area code number I didn't recognize.

"Excuse me," I said and took the call. It was the man sitting opposite me telling me he needed to see me urgently and would be at my office at ten A.M. unless he heard from me.

"Let me guess." I ended the call and gazed across the desk at the gentleman. "You're Christopher Marks?"

He nodded. "You just got the message? I called last night." He leaned across the desk, peering at my phone.

"Don't!" I barked. "This is a crime scene. Let's go across the road and talk."

"Maybe the bad weather screwed up the cell phone signal," he said.

"Yeah." I wondered how many other calls I'd missed, but I didn't want to scroll through my phone in front of him.

As much as I wondered why my being gay helped him in his inquiry, I didn't want to discuss things here until I'd had a chance to go over the office and check what else was missing. I escorted him out the door and locked it, not that it mattered. Somebody had already been able to get in without any trouble.

We took the stairs down to the front of the building. Rain still came down in soft sheets, and I was surprised when Christopher Marks opened up a small, black umbrella. I pulled the slicker hood over my head and gestured to

O'Brien's Irish Pub across the road on the southwest corner.

"A bar?" he looked askance. "It's a little early for alcohol, isn't it?"

"Must be cocktail hour somewhere in the world," I joked. He didn't smile back.

"They make coffee," I shouted as rain started pouring down again.

We dashed across the street against the lights and made it inside. The cheery warmth of the place lifted my spirits, and apparently Christopher's since he was now smiling. The place was packed. Every last stool at the bar had been taken, and the tables scattered around the room were filled. We grabbed the last remaining corner table. Since it only had one chair, I offered it to my potential client and scurried off to find a second chair. I scrounged one from a large group and returned to find Christopher placidly studying the food menu.

"They have seven dollar lunch specials," he said. "My treat. How do you feel about fish and chips? You look like you could use a good meal. "

I would have objected except that he was right. The over-head TV behind the bar that boasted an obscenely large collection of Irish Whiskey variations blared over the chatter. The weather was rotten, according to the news report. With a chance of getting much, much worse.

"Fish and chips sounds good," I said. As the waiter rushed over to us, he kept an eye on the rowdy table beside us. We made quick work of our orders. We both wanted the special, and we each wanted coffee.

"It's my son," Christopher burst out as soon as the waiter dashed away again. "He's missing."

Christopher's eyes adopted the hooded look I'd seen so many times before, both as a cop and as a private investigator. The anguish of not knowing what has happened to a loved one, especially a child. I doubt in life there could be anything worse.

I sat back and waited a beat, but he didn't say anything more.

"Is he gay?" I asked, keeping my tone gentle.

He nodded. "Look, I wasn't supposed to say anything because I know you don't advertise and that you work from referrals only, but I ah . . ." He broke off his sentence, a muscle working in his cheek. I could see the shadows under his eyes now. Over his left shoulder, I could make out the tall, bulky frame of my pal, Looky Hendrix. Poor bastard was having a tough time of things lately. He'd been one of the most successful rock singers in the U.S. in the seventies and eighties. Now, in his late sixties, he should have been enjoying his declining years. Instead, he'd broken up with his cover band, his latest wife had left him and in a spectacularly embarrassing court hearing earlier that morning had lost his driving privileges for life.

I glanced at his leg. He was wearing an ankle monitor. It looked ridiculous with the bottom of his black leather pants tucked around it. A guy, a third of his age, couldn't get away with all the leather Looky wore. His home-dyed black hair stuck up in spikes that looked sad on his tired face.

On the TV above, there was a recap of his court sentencing. Christopher turned to see what I was watching, and it was painful to look at poor Looky on the TV being berated by the judge who called him a menace to society.

I had no idea what the hell Looky would do now without the ability to drive. He relied on each and every gig he took, bad as he performed these days. He raised his whiskey glass to himself on the TV above. He dropped the glass on the counter and turned to leave. His kohl-rimmed eyes were leaking black rivers down his face. Alice Cooper come undone.

11

He walked past us, giving me a nod. He stunk of booze and cigarettes.

"Christ, he makes me feel old," Christopher commented when the door banged shut behind Looky.

"Me, too," I said.

"I used to listen to his band." Christopher seemed to be in pain. He shook out his shoulders. "Actually, I loved them. My son hated their music." At the mention of his son, his face twisted in grief.

"Tell me about him." Part of my job is being amateur psychiatrist. Of course, I needed details about the guy if I was supposed to find him. At least, I assumed I was supposed to find him.

"Dane is a good man." He let out a sigh and looked around for the waiter. "I could use that cup of coffee." He licked his lips. I saw the waiter shouldering his way through a mess of people playing darts. He arrived with our meals and our coffees, looking agitated.

"I've been complaining for months about having the early shift," the waiter told us as he deposited cream and sugar bowls on the table. "I prayed for days like this. Now I'm rapidly losing the will to live."

The look on Christopher's face alarmed me. I thought the man was going to have a heart attack.

When the waiter took off, I said, "What's going on with Dane?"

"My son is very depressed." He doctored his coffee and picked up his cup. He took a sip, pulling a face. "This is horrible."

"You put salt in it instead of sugar."

"I did?" He looked flustered and confused. Outside, the rain began beating down so hard we could hear it. For a moment, everyone stopped talking.

"Oh, man, where do I start?" Christopher took my coffee,

added sugar and stirred. He stared off thoughtfully in the middle distance, and I waited. "I guess things went bad for him" — He winced at the word bad — "when the studio let go of him three years ago."

"Studio?"

"He was the head of the art department at Alamo Studios. He was earning great money. He did all their movie posters, their DVD cases. He won awards. He'd been there for eighteen years, and he won awards. Lots and lots of awards."

Yes, Christopher had already mentioned that, but a distraught father is wont to repeat things under duress.

"They let go of him. They couldn't afford him anymore. They brought in younger kids, but these days, these guys aren't artists! They're computer geeks who use Photoshop and think it makes them Rembrandt."

He sipped his coffee. I waited.

"At first, they gave him some of the bigger accounts on a freelance basis. I had no idea he was starting to struggle with his bills. He called me one night, frantic. He was worried he was going to lose his house. I love my son, and he's never given me or his mother a moment of worry. Until he lost his job."

His voice trembled. I was starting to feel very bad for Dane Marks.

"He borrowed money from us. Well, we gave it to him to pay his mortgage for a few months. He said he'd pay it back, but that was his decision, not ours."

"Did he pay it back?"

He nodded. "And then he got quiet, and my wife suggested I come out here to visit him."

"Where do you live?"

"Austin, Texas."

"Do your wife and son not get along?"

"No, no. They're close, but he's more open with me. She

took his sexuality hard. It's usually the other way around from what I understand, but I have a gay brother, and I never wanted my son to feel alienated. I've seen what my brother's been through. My wife is looking after her father. He has Alzheimer's and lives with us. Anyway, I came out here, and Dane admitted he was working in the gay porn industry."

"As a performer?"

He shook his head. "As a director." He drained his cup, and I caught the waiter's eye. He came over with the coffee pot and looked at our untouched food.

"Everybody says the chips are too crispy. I'll get you replacements." He refilled Christopher's cup.

"The chips are fine," Christopher said, but the waiter ignored him.

"Can I get a fresh cup, please?" I asked, earning a look that would have smelted metal from the waiter. He snatched up our plates and the coffee and took off.

"I have no judgment about porn," Christopher said. "Dane liked the work, and he was grateful to be making money, but . . ."

After a significant pause, I said, gently, "But?"

"He works very hard to produce innovative, original sex scenes." The man blushed. "He's actually won awards for his porn movies, too." He gave me a swift, ironic smile.

"Why do I sense another but?" I asked.

He stared into his coffee cup, his thumb running across the same spot over and over along the rim. "Somebody told the studio he was directing gay porn and it's killed his career."

I squinted at him. "What?"

He nodded. "I know, right?" He blew out an agonized breath.

I stared at him a moment. "I don't understand. Does he direct under his own name?"

"No. He works as Danny Dark."

I knew the name. Hell, I'd seen most of Dark's movies. He worked for Bay City, a major gay porn company and, yeah, his work was popular. He'd dared do the unthinkable. He'd introduced the word *plot* into his movies. His name had started showing up a few years ago. People either loved or hated his movies. What was indisputable was that Danny Dark had discovered some hot talent and had an eye for good-looking models.

"Is he handsome?" I asked Christopher.

"He's attractive. Not handsome enough to be a model, frankly, but he's cute. He keeps in shape." He fell silent again.

My thoughts raced. Looks were no barrier to getting work in gay porn, but I was a gay man and knew that our people revered their porn stars in a way that straight people didn't. I knew that it placed unrealistic expectations for younger men to have perfect bodies and sensational porn star sex all day long. The industry was rife with drug abuse.

"Does he have a drug problem?" I asked.

"He didn't used to. Not before he got into porn. Then, he started having problems."

"Heck," I said. "I knew some of the models had trouble getting work because of porn, but the directors?"

He nodded. "He had a lover who worked at Alamo Studios. It was his idea that Dane start directing gay porn. When the studio called Dane, saying they had a possible new position for him a few months ago, he went in to meet with them. He was so excited. I was so proud of him. He never gave up. And then. All hell broke loose."

"What happened?"

"His ex told the studio about Dane's other career, and they blasted him saying they couldn't have somebody like that in their company. One of the executives, mind you, asked Dane to send him a copy of his latest DVD saying he was a fan but couldn't admit to it publicly."

Well," I said, "Ain't that a kick in the head?"

Christopher said nothing. He just stared at the floor.

"What did Dane do?"

Christopher looked up at me. "He tried to kill himself. Twice."

I stared at him. "Oh, my God!"

The devastated father in front of me fought the emotion he'd been keeping in all morning.

"I don't know where . . . what to do. He lost his house two months ago. We simply didn't have the money to pay for it. He was upside down on his mortgage. He owed more than the house was worth. The bank wouldn't work with him, especially when they found out how he made his income.

"Losing his home has really affected him. He moved into an apartment, and I got a phone call a month ago from his landlord telling me Dane had taken an overdose of sleeping pills. He almost died. I flew straight out here–"

His voice broke off.

"What happened when you arrived?"

"My son was in terrible shape. The gay porn industry isn't what it used to be. Bay City was sold, and they owed him money. The new owners think people like Dane are dinosaurs. He got scraps. A scene here, a scene there. The hot new thing is gay porn stars creating their own companies and controlling everything. It's all subscription services now. Illegal downloads, piracy, those things killed the big companies."

"You know a lot about it."

"I made it my business to know. My son was very innovative in his approach. He created his own small company within Bay City, and it drove a lot of business to the big, parent company, but he never saw a dime from it. The new owners said it wasn't their problem. There wasn't anything we could do."

He lapsed into silent despair for a moment. Then he said, "DVDs no longer sell. Not the way they used to. The studios sell sex scenes now, and they're pirated all over the Internet within hours."

Christopher looked at me, putting his cup down. "Last week, Dane tried to take his own life again. I had to go home. My wife's been ill, and I was out here for a month. As soon as I left for the airport, he swallowed a bunch of pills again. I flew back out here the next day. He was committed to a seventy-two-hour hold. He got out again, but he's really bad. Severely depressed. He disappeared two days ago, and I have no idea where to find him. I don't know where to even start looking."

Tears fell down his cheeks now. "I love my son more than anything in the world, and I know this time he's going to go someplace where I can't find him. He's going to kill himself."

The waiter made an inopportune return appearance.

"I just realized I never brought your food and I feel bad about that." He glanced at the sobbing Christopher. "Boy, he must be really hungry."

I shook my head. The waiter was smart enough to realize he'd blundered into a private and terrible moment.

He held up a hand. "Coffee's on me," he said, backing away.

I waited for Christopher to pull himself together. The truth was, I felt wretched for the guy. With love like this, love I'd personally never known from a parent, I wondered how Dane could even think of taking his own life.

His father looked up at me, his face a map of grief.

"Matt, I love my son. If he dies, I die. I just want him to be happy. I want him to know that love isn't just for sale. Love is all there is. He can find it. I just want him to hang on."

He hung his head and covered his face with his hands. "I want my little boy to believe in dreams again."

# CHAPTER TWO

Dane Marks had rented an apartment in the Village Green district of Los Angeles, close to the house he lost in Baldwin Hills. When I learned that both suburbs belonged to the Southwest Community Police Division, I had a pretty good idea how Christopher Marks got my number.

And why.

"When Dane tried to take his own life last week, the reason he survived was that apparently his CD player was stuck on the same song for hours," Christopher told me.

"His neighbors went mad when he wouldn't turn it down. They knew he was home because his car was in his parking space. They left phone messages, a note on the door. The landlord let himself in with his keys and found him unconscious on the floor."

We walked down the street in a rare moment of ceasefire from the relentless rain as Christopher said that the police had arrived because apparently, the hospital notified them regarding the high volume of drugs he'd consumed.

"They thought he was some kind of drug dealer. I'm surprised Dane survived the second overdose, but he wasn't well. His second attempt really affected him. I don't know where he got the drugs, but he had all kinds of things in his system. He came home, and he was a shell of himself. He was subdued for a few days, and then he seemed to be getting a bit better. One morning he said he was going to the gym to work out. I was so relieved. I thought that was a really good sign, but he never came back."

At a crosswalk, Christopher looked agitated again. "I have his laptop and a couple of other things you may need to help you in your inquiries. Detective Gressing of the vice squad was really nice to me."

"I suspected he was the one who suggested you call me," I said.

Christopher flushed guiltily. "Aw heck. I wasn't supposed to mention that."

I shrugged. My ex might have abandoned our love ship, but he made up for it with frequent referrals.

"When my son disappeared he told me there wasn't much they could do. I kept pushing, and he suggested I contact you."

We walked to his car, which was parked on 22nd Street. He unlocked the trunk and handed me a sports bag. "It's got his laptop, and I've made lists of his friends' names. I have a spare copy of his apartment key here."

"Where did he live in Baldwin Hills?"

"I wrote the address down in the list I gave you. That was the first place the police went to. I thought he might go there to die. He loved that place."

"Has the bank sold it?"

"Not yet. My son was in litigation with them. It's been horrendous. They don't care how many lives they ruin. He wasn't even that far behind on his mortgage. Four months. But then they slapped on fines and fees, and it quickly got out of his reach."

He stared at the car. "I have to fly back to Austin. My wife is very sick. She has diverticulitis. I don't think this has helped at all." He put his hands on the trunk of his car.

For a moment, I thought he might be having a heart attack the way his body seemed to be shaking and twitching.

"Oh, God," he said. "I'm grateful you met with me. Here's enough money to get you started." He reached into the trunk and handed me an envelope filled with cash.

"You kept this in here?" I couldn't believe it.

He shrugged. "It's got a pretty good alarm." He banged the trunk shut. "I have a three o'clock flight out of Long Beach back to Austin. I'm flying Jet Blue." He shook his head. "I have to go all the way to damned Long Beach. They don't fly to Austin from any of the other airports. So I have some downtime before my flight.

"You have my contact numbers. I'd appreciate updates as often as possible. Please don't worry about how ... seamy the information might seem. I need answers, and I need them before my wife, and I drop dead from the insane panic we're experiencing."

I couldn't help myself. I hugged the guy. I heard a bone creaking in his back and shrank away guiltily.

He waved it off. "My back's out. I feel like crap, but nothing matters but getting my son back." He gestured toward the envelope. "There's three thousand dollars in there. Let me know when you need more."

I suspected he'd given me what he could afford and I hoped I wouldn't be needing more.

"Gotta return this rental by one," he said.

With the rain about to come down again, I didn't fancy his chances but didn't say so. I walked back to my office. Crime scene or no I had to get to work on my missing persons case.

My first call was to Stu Gressing. I thanked him for the referral.

"Nobody's more qualified, sweet—I mean, Matt."

"Did you meet Dane Marks?" I asked him. Old habits died hard. Too damned hard. I wanted to scream like a prom queen. *"You like me! You still like me!"*

"Yeah. He was sick as shit. I saw him in the hospital, then briefly at his apartment. I think he was embarrassed about all the attention. I don't think this guy was crying for help. I really think he was trying to check outta here."

I paused for a moment. I couldn't get access to Dane's computer files. Encrypted. Encoded. Annoying.

My go-to computer guy was Looky's son, Angus, who lived with his father, or maybe it was the other way around. I thought of Angus as my brother, considering we'd grown up together. When I called Looky, however, he told me Angus had moved out and gave me his new number.

"How are you doing?" I asked, more to be polite than anything.

"I've seen better days," he said and ended the call.

His son evidently had, too, because he seemed all too keen to make a quick fifty bucks, more than any nineteen-year-old computer geek should have been.

He came to my office thirty minutes later, and it immediately struck me how much he looked like his father. Looky had been a handsome, strapping guy until the drugs, drink, and dissipation got to him.

Angus had always been a friendly, funny guy in spite of his unorthodox upbringing, but he was sullen now. No jokes, no banter. He sat in my office chair and flicked a glance at his surroundings.

"Going for the Kabuki modern look, are we?"

He didn't seem to want a response. He bent his head to his task. "Guy who owns this isn't the trusting type. There are three different codes on here. I take it you want me to get rid of them all?"

"Yes, please."

He kept working. "Might take a while. Got anything else to do except breathing down my neck?

Boy, somebody was touchy today.

"What's going on?" I asked him. I'd never seen Angus so pissed.

"I caught my dad screwing my girlfriend." His head dropped. For the second time that day I watched a grown man cry. Looky looked like shit. Who'd the hell bang him?

"Your girlfriend? Is she blind?"

"No. A fan. She used me to get to him." He shrugged off my hand as I put it on his shoulder.

"When did you move out?"

"Last night, right after I came in and found them in his bed. He said it was an accident." He was devastated, in spite of his flippant tone. He frowned. "Why do people say that? You don't accidentally slip and fall into a woman's pussy."

"He meant it was a mistake." I tried to keep my tone gentle. I really wanted to kick Looky's ass. I would have if I thought it would do any good. I'd known Angus since he was born. Looky and I went that far back. I was only ten years older than Angus, but I suddenly felt ancient. Looky, my former guitar hero, had gone off the deep end this time for sure. Typical addict, he'd done the one thing to alienate his last close relationship. He'd isolated himself so he could die alone.

I glanced at the computer.

*Shit. Just like Dane Marks.*

"Fuck that," Angus spat out. "He'd ball anything. Did it have to be *my* chick?"

"I'm gonna check on something," I said. "I won't be long. If you crack the code, can you call me?"

"Not if, when, Matt. I never met a code I couldn't break."

"Perfect. So call me. And don't answer the phone."

He laughed. "You're expecting a call?"

"I'm a private investigator. I'm always expecting calls."

His laugh turned nasty. I turned my back and walked out the door.

The weather held as I took a quick drive to Baldwin Hills. People had been so housebound they took to the freeways, their vehicles hydroplaning dangerously. I was a veteran of the Los Angeles freeway system, but my hands shook as I took the turnoff on the 405 South.

I wanted to get a feel for Dane Marks. His house, the one he'd lost, was in the deep bosom of what was often referred to as the "Black Beverly Hills." Known mostly as the original site for the Olympic Games Village back in 1932, it was also the home of several wealthy celebrities who preferred reality for their children over the fakery of the real Beverly Hills. It also had an unusual, unattractive sideshow going on; tons and tons of oil wells dotted the district. Active drilling took place, which wouldn't have made the area an appealing proposition for me.

Nestled on a corner lot of Sunlight Place, Dane's former home changed all my thoughts about that. A huge, mid-century modern, three-bedroom, two bathroom house, the bank had a pending bid on the property that had been valued at half a million dollars. According to the stats I pulled up on my cell phone, it had received two offers, both above the asking price.

I let out a whistle as I read that piece of information.

Stepping across the rain-soaked grass, I took in the gigantic bougainvillea that stood out front. The rain had beaten it, its stooping branches reminding me of Angus's hunched shoulders. I looked in the windows. Hardwood floors. Fireplaces in every room. It was chic, comfortable and yet spoke of money, too. I had a feeling Dane had sunk a small fortune into his upgrades.

The backyard was the biggest surprise. He'd left a couple of wicker armchairs on the covered back porch. They'd been painted the same pink that dominated the garden. It was a wonderland of color. I could hear water dropping in steady beats from the gutters and wondered how many times he'd sat in one of his chairs staring out at his secret world.

I was able to get into the backyard via an unlocked gate. The back sliding doors to the house revealed a pristine, ready-to-move-in home that would be anybody's pride and joy. I turned back to the armchairs. They looked expensive. Why had he left them there?

For a moment, I pondered the question and took a seat. From where I perched on the damp cushion, I had a perfect view of the entire garden and the surrounding trees. Maybe he couldn't take the chairs because they wouldn't fit or wouldn't work in his new apartment.

Maybe he'd left them as a gift for the new owners.

No. I had it now.

He was an artist. He couldn't bear the thought of breaking up his unique and utterly exquisite tableau.

I walked around the front of the house, noticing the locked box on the door handle. Traces of the Marshals' eviction notice hadn't been entirely scraped from the antique wooden door. I gazed up and down the leafy street. Beautiful. All I needed was Wally and the Beaver to stop by for a game of pick-up, and my trip back to 1950s Americana would be complete.

Moving back to my car, I felt just a little of the despair, the hopelessness, that Dane Marks had felt when he left his house for the last time.

Inside the vehicle, I called Angus on his cell phone. "He's a mad fucker, this Dane Marks," Angus announced. "I got one code down, the other still to go." I could hear him cracking his knuckles.

"I thought there were three codes."

"There are only two. The third was a fake. A very cool trick. I'm impressed."

"Good news. One more stop to make," I said. "Then I'm heading back."

Rain came in a mild burst as I headed to Village Green,

the historic mid-century garden community developed in Baldwin Hills around 1940. Now declared a National Historic Landmark, I saw a trend in Dane's taste. His rented digs in the original Village Green complex painted white with pale green trim would please his artistic eye.

His apartment, shielded behind a long wooden walkway with succulents growing on either side of the path, looked kind of nondescript to me. Boring. Depressing. I'd rapidly lose the will to live myself, stuck in one of these places.

I unlocked his door and walked in. I could smell the slight scent of something. Aftershave? Deodorant? The compact, dark quarters must have seemed cave-like to the man who'd previously lived in a house on a street called Sunlight Place.

Everything in his apartment shrieked gay. From the huge black and white photos of hot, handsome men, to his collection of photos of himself with numerous gay superstars, I took in the outward showings of a fabulous life.

He was handsome in a blond, boy-next-door way. I had to disagree with his father's proclamation that he wasn't handsome enough to perform in a gay porn movie.

Dane was handsome but didn't play up his good looks. I studied a photo of Dane with gay porn impresario Michael Lucas. The man was pouting. Come to think of it, it was Lucas's trademark pose.

In each of the photos, Dane smiled but didn't look happy. In his bedroom, I found an empty iPad box but no iPad.

His bathroom medicine cabinet revealed a frightening number of empty medicine bottles for some pretty intense tranquilizers. I jotted down the names of the drugstores where he'd picked up his prescriptions and wondered how he'd managed to get such huge quantities of the same pills. Provisions were in place these days via computer systems to prevent this sort of pill hoarding.

My cell phone rang. "Cracked it," Angus said, sounding

smug. I noticed a cat's dishes on the floor and stared. No food. No water.

"I'm on my way back," I told him. I took a quick look around and wondered where Dane's father had been sleeping in the one bedroom apartment. It felt cold. Sterile. I also wondered whether he'd put stuff in storage.

As I drove back to the office, I called Christopher Marks.

"Does Dane have a cat?" I asked him.

"He did. She disappeared right after he first moved into that apartment. We think she got out through an open window. He took it awfully hard. She was his baby. You know . . ." I heard the crack in Christopher's voice and his sharp intake of breath. "I don't think he would have even tried to kill himself if that cat was still with him. I think she was the last thing he had that felt real."

I let that sink in for a moment.

"What have you found out?" Christopher asked.

"I just cracked his computer code. I should have some news soon."

"Very good." He sounded pleased. "I'm stuck here in Long Beach Airport. The flight's been delayed a couple of hours."

"I'll be in touch," I promised.

I made it back to the office. Angus was asleep with his feet on the desk. He yawned as I walked in. "I'd offer you coffee," I told him, but somebody swiped my Keurig."

"Bummer. I've always wanted one of those." He yawned again. "I got through his codes. He has a rotating list of six that kick into place each time the computer is shut down. I wrote 'em all out for you. I haven't had a good look at it yet. I wanted to wait for you.

"Jee-zus!" he suddenly yelled, leaning back in my office chair as if the computer had fritzed him. I moved behind the chair to look over his shoulder. What I saw threatened to give me a monster boner.

What Angus saw made him screw his eyes up tight as if it would make the image of a hot, hung naked guy being used as a screensaver go away.

"Gross," Angus muttered. He kept typing. "Here. You're lucky. Apart from millions of nude men, the guy who owns this computer has synced it to his iPad and cell phone. What goes into those winds up here."

He showed me a few cool tricks and then held out his hand. I gave him a hundred bucks.

"Thanks, Matt. This is the nicest thing that's happened to me all day."

He moved out of the chair, sliding the money into his wallet. "She's left him now, according to the text message she sent me. Guess she'd never seen what an asshole Dad is when he's been on a bender."

"Where are you staying?"

He lifted his shoulders. "Slept in my car last night in the parking garage on third. I just paid the rent on Dad's apartment for the month, so I'm broke until payday."

"You can stay with me if you like. You know, until things get settled."

He frowned. "With you and that crazy cat? The one that wee-wees on everything?"

"Yeah."

"Thanks. I'll stick to my car."

*Whatever.* I waited until he'd gone and studied the computer. It was filled with tons of images of models, nude and otherwise. I checked the time on the toolbar. Just after one. I had a lot of work to do.

By five o'clock, when Christopher Marks was scheduled to fly out, I'd made a lot of progress. Dane's entire life was on the computer. He'd apparently been syncing all his iPad and cell phone activities to his computer because photos uploaded to his iPad that had transferred to his laptop within the past few hours kept popping up in his email inbox.

His emails revealed a lot. He'd been on Hotwire, an Internet service that shops the best prices on anything to do with travel. He'd been looking for flights to Miami, and I was thankful he had Gmail because I could read his emails but save them as "new." If he was checking his account, he'd never know I'd been snooping around.

Two of his most recent messages had come from gay porn models I knew by name. Rowdy St. Claire and Anthony Chase had both written to him asking if he was going to the GPN Awards in Miami. Chase joked that Danny Dark was up for an award.

*Are you coming? Don't keep us in the dark, Danny!*

Dane's Hotwire account was also easy to access. I could see he'd been looking for an airfare and hotel combination booking. From what I could tell he wasn't fussy about where he stayed.

What intrigued me more was that he seemed to have been making contact with two other models that, as far as I knew, he'd never worked with. I checked his bio on the Internet Movie Database. Nope. He'd never worked with either of the two men. They seemed different from his usual models. Beefier, more macho. One of them seemed familiar. I studied his face and was surprised to see that it was a model I'd watched and frankly been attracted to in several movies. None of them had been Danny Dark productions.

I was certain that the model now going by Thomas Conrad had previously worked as Tommy Terrell. He'd grown his hair out, developed some body hair, which was not popular in the current porn trend and added some bulk to his tall frame.

When I checked Tommy Terrell's Twitter account, he'd

announced he was retiring from porn to focus on escorting. His Twitter account hadn't been updated for several months, but I Googled him and found he was registered on rentboy.com.

*Escorting.*

I doubled back and checked the emails again. I Googled Thomas Conrad and, sure enough, he was the former Tommy Terrell. His Twitter account was filled with inane updates about his diet, muscle-building supplements and his aspirations for a mainstream movie career. When people tweeted to him about his gay porn career, he'd respond viciously that he no longer acknowledged Tommy Terrell's existence. Why hadn't he shut down the Tommy Terrell account? Maybe he still got messages there. Maybe he'd go back some day to being Tommy Terrell who had fourteen thousand followers. Thomas Conrad had two hundred. I studied his more recent photos. He certainly looked different enough to pass as somebody other than Tommy Terrell, but I'd picked him out in a matter of minutes.

Checking through Google, I saw that he was modeling out of Miami and, according to his Rentboy.com profile, he was available for nude dates. Sex would only happen if he liked the guy. That's what his notes actually said. His cell phone number was listed and, apparently, he was on call twenty-four hours a day.

His nude photos had me salivating. He had a beautiful cock, and I was pleased to see that hadn't changed. He was still hung like a rhinoceros. I kept staring at him. I jotted down his cell phone number, then ran the second model's name through the Internet.

This model was also a big guy. Italian-looking. Ricky Stanton. Again he worked out of Miami. I was surprised when I checked back on Gmail and saw that Dane had received email confirmation of a first class ticket to Miami on American Airlines. He'd also paid for a suite at the swish

Mandarin Oriental Hotel. The host hotel for the awards was the Hyatt. But he'd booked an even more expensive place to stay.

Fine by me. As long as he stayed alive until I got there. I began searching for flights when an email came in twenty seconds later from Thomas Conrad.

*Hey. Tried leaving you a voicemail but your messages are full. I'll be at your hotel tonight. Let me know what room. I don't do drugs. If you need something to take the edge off like you said, Ricky can help.*

I stared at the message. It was a text that had been duplicated on Dane's emails.

For a moment I felt jubilant that Dane was still alive and arranging some kind of sexual tryst with the two models. I clicked back over to his reservation page.

A dark and disturbing thought had occurred to me.

This was a man who was severely depressed. Suicidal. Broke.

A picture was beginning to emerge, and I didn't like it very much. He was throwing caution and his finances out the fucking window.

He was going to Miami to have one last blowout party.

He'd booked a couple of models and asked one of them to bring drugs.

Dane Marks was obviously planning on going out with a bang.

It was one way to go, I suppose.

It wasn't pleasant breaking the news of my leave-taking to Ronin. The cat just stared at me. I tried to explain I needed the work. I needed to feed him. I had no idea how long I'd be gone, I told him. He just yawned in my face.

When my cell phone rang, I checked the readout. It was Christopher Marks returning my call. I told him everything I knew. He was stunned to learn of his son's travel plans.

"He's maxing out his credit card by the sound of it," he said. "At least we know he's still alive."

"I'm flying to Miami on a flight that leaves at ten o'clock tonight. One hour after he leaves."

"Keep me posted," he said. "I'm stuck here at Long Beach. The flight's been delayed another hour. Or so they claim."

"Sorry to hear it. I'll be in touch. Please try not to worry." A moment later my cell phone rang again. It was Angus.

"Is that offer of a place to stay still good?"

"Sure it is." I'd been about to put the bite on my neighbor to feed the King of Pee, but this was even better.

"I'm going out of town," I told him. "You'd better come over so I can give you a key and show you around."

"Be right there," he said.

When he arrived, he carted in a computer bag, a couple of guitars and a duffle bag.

"I have more stuff in the car. "Does your cat wee-wee on everything?"

"Only if you leave it on the floor."

"Good to know." He peered at my small overnight bag sitting on the dining table. "Where you off to, Matty?"

"Miami."

"Must be nice."

"Not really. It's work. Missing person."

"Dane Marks, the computer guy?"

I nodded.

"Shit. I'd love to be missing. Listen. Have you ever thought about what would have happened if your mom and my dad had actually gotten married? If they'd actually made it work?"

"Yeah." I hated to admit it. I'd thought about it a lot. I pride myself, or maybe I was kidding myself, that my mother was the one woman Looky had really loved. When I was ten and Angus was a newborn, my mom, a backup singer for Looky's band and a ton of others had been the hottest woman in the biz.

Some of the performers fought over her, but it hadn't surprised me that Looky snapped her up. He'd had a devilish on-stage persona, but off it was a smart, well-read guy. He loved kids and his wife had up and left him and their newborn son and their five-year-old daughter.

It had turned out she was in rehab. She'd overdosed in a mad fit of rebellion and Looky got stuck with the kids.

My mom fell so hard and fast for him it gave me whiplash when we moved into his Cadillac Avenue house. I just loved the name of the place. He adored my mom, and for a while, things were fantastic between them. Then she started drinking to keep him company, and he was a rotten-mean drunk. He was also a druggie, and a whore and their fights became epic.

By the time I'd turned fifteen, I'd moved out to live with my dad, who didn't want kids. He especially didn't want a gay son. Ironically, my mom left Looky. I moved back in with him and took care of Angus and his sister Amelia, turning a blind eye to Looky's endless parade of women.

Looky actually loved his kids and kept working to support them, but I moved out when I was seventeen when Looky had a bitch-on-wheels move in. She hated me. She hated Angus and Amelia. The kids ended up in boarding school. I ended up alone. Again. Naturally.

Looky ended up married and divorced, losing most of his money to his scheming new wife.

Yeah, I'd thought about how things might have been, but I'd blocked all these thoughts, these pain-laden memories, for years.

My mother had never come back to herself after Looky got through with her. I missed her terribly, but she was off in some ashram in India following some guru. I didn't miss that mother. I missed the one who backed up Nancy Sinatra on stage and went shopping with her most Saturdays. The mom who made cool muffins on Sunday mornings with melted jellybeans and marshmallows inside them.

Looky had alienated everyone, including the daughter who'd always loved and adored him, and now he'd punished his son anew.

I felt so bad for Angus, who sat on my sofa looking like I was his last friend.

Perhaps I was. Looky had a way of annihilating everyone who came close. I gave Angus the keys with stern instructions not to let Ronin out of the front door.

"He can go on the balcony only if you're here. He likes to sleep in the sun."

"No chance of that happening any time soon."

I showed him Ronin's food bowls and explained his finicky ways.

"Go." Angus sounded tired. "He's a cat. We'll survive."

"I need one more favor." Wait. What was I saying? I was doing him the favor.

"What?" he asked, his tone only slightly bored.

"Can I sync everything on the computer with my iPad?"

"No. It's synced with his. You run the risk of him getting an encryption alert."

"Okay." I'd have to take the damned thing with me. I finished packing in silence.

Angus was lying asleep on the sofa, the cat curled up on his feet, as I came out of the bedroom with a small overnight bag.

"Hussy," I told Ronin. I tried petting his head, but he just swatted at me.

Nice. It was the story of my life.

# CHAPTER THREE

I didn't really have a game plan for what I'd do once I got to Miami at six o'clock the next morning. I didn't think the Mandarin Oriental would allow such early check-in, but I suspected that the Hyatt, the host hotel for the awards, would be alive and kicking. Probably most participants would be showing up today at some point since the awards were taking place that night.

The city might have been officially still waking up, but Miami seemed like a giant block party, even at the airport. I didn't need to visit the baggage carousels since I'd carried my bag on board, but I did want to check out the arrivals section. I wasn't disappointed to see numerous famous names in gay porn picking up their suitcases.

These guys didn't travel light.

I followed a gaggle of familiar faces, trying to stick close to them. As the pneumatic doors opened, I almost fell over from the heat. Man, it was hot outside. I sweated in the humidity as I followed a group onto a hotel shuttle heading to the Hyatt.

"Sorry," the driver announced, not looking at all like he was, "The AC's busted." We all groaned. Squeezing in beside a bunch of new arrivals for the gay porn awards, I was shocked at how many women were in the line-up of guests.

Outside the increasingly warm van, the city was hopping. *Party like there's no tomorrow* seemed to be the theme. A stark contrast with Los Angeles that seemed to shut down by ten and waken around nine the following morning.

The crew in my van was noisy and funny. And oh God, so bitchy.

"Is Chris Carter coming to Miami?" asked Gio Gomez, one of the hottest guys I've ever seen on camera or off.

"No. He retired, didn't you hear?" said another performer whose face was familiar but I couldn't recall his name.

"Retired?" Gio looked surprised. "Again?"

"Yeah. It's hard to find cocks big enough to fill his gaping *man*gina in the real world," twittered a twink, making everyone roar with laughter.

"Not really retired," another one said. "Renting itself in Rentboy.com."

"Isn't everybody?" Gio deadpanned.

It went on and on.

"What about that ingrate Terry Tyler?" another said. "Doing bareback now. Guess he wants to die."

They were hilarious, inane and so vicious I thanked God they didn't know me. I was certain if they did, the moment my back was turned they'd gossip about me, too.

"What about John Magnum?" somebody shouted from the back of the van. "He's doing straight porn now."

This was the scourge of the gay porn industry. Straight men who went gay-for-pay and swung back and forth, desperate for money. The conversation ran in circles about who was gay, who was straight, who was bi. Was there even such a thing as bi? This was a fascinating topic discussion at the best of times, and some of the observations seemed insightful.

I recognized immediately one of the people sitting as a director and videographer. He went by the name Mistress Kate but wasn't dressed as a woman now. He was dressed like a man. One that had been bashed more than once with the ugly stick.

There were several well-known porn stars who all seemed

drunk. One guy was busy lamenting the fact that he'd vowed to kick doing gay porn but couldn't make a go of his financial planning business.

I stared at him a moment, wondering if he was joking. I was particularly fascinated by him because he was a well-known bottom in gay porn and he was accompanied by his *wife*. As in, an actual woman. Suddenly, the whole bisexual discussion seemed both awkward and downright cruel. I watched his wife sitting there smiling as her husband made out with a Cuban porn star known for his gigantic, uncut cock.

She grabbed a camera from her Céline Nano purse. I couldn't take my eyes off that damned thing. I knew for a fact it retailed for around seventeen hundred bucks. I knew this because my last case involved a nasty divorce over one of those purses. The husband in question had purchased one as a gift. His wife found it, assumed it was for her and was surprised when he gave her a toaster for her birthday instead.

It had been my job to track down the recipient of that Céline Nano. I didn't have to look far. After following the husband for half a day, I watched him coming out of his office late in the afternoon accompanied by a hot young woman toting the um . . . tote. I took a few photos and followed them to a skeezy motel on La Cienega. Yeah, he could blow two grand on a purse but wouldn't spend more than thirty bucks on a room.

He was about to lose a lot more than that. His wife saw the photos and flipped out. I would too had I been her. It hit her hard to learn her husband was sticking it to *her* personal assistant . . .

I tried not to stare at the married bottom, and the Cuban top flipped each other's cocks out of their pants and sucked each other briefly.

The shuttle driver didn't react. Nobody did. I tried to act nonchalant. She took photos of her hubby, who promised the Cuba she'd post the photos on his website as soon as they got to his room.

The two men were all over one another. The Cuban was there with his boyfriend, who, when nobody but me seemed to be watching, lapsed into the kind of glum silence I'd seen a lot lately.

"We're rivals for the award for best cock in the biz," the famous bottom told me. "Who do you think should win?"

"He should." I pointed to the Cuban. Everybody roared with laughter. The Cuban leaned into me when I said, "I'm a fan." He claimed my mouth in a deep kiss that left me dizzy. I felt like quoting Angus. It was the nicest thing that had happened to me all day.

We arrived at the hotel, and I followed the crowd once again, slipping the van driver a buck for hauling my bag on and off the vehicle. I wasn't sure exactly where Dane Marks was, but since it was now six-twenty, I had a feeling it might be too early for him to check into his suite at the Mandarin Oriental.

I took out my cell phone as I entered the packed lobby, absorbing the wild scene around me. Every single genre in gay porn was well represented. And then some. A famous Dom was verbally abusing what I assumed was his sub for not putting his collar back on in a timely fashion.

"I lost the padlock key," the sub bleated. "They went through my bag at security."

"You should have put your collar back on during the flight."

"I couldn't," the sub said. "I told you, I lost the padlock key." I wasn't sure who I felt sorrier for, but my money was on a painful outcome for the sub. I retreated to a far wall, grabbed one of the luxurious leather armchairs and plugged in Dane's laptop. I had to subscribe to a local Internet provider and began hunting for one when, joy, the hotel's Internet server kicked in. I accessed Dane's emails.

Three new messages.

I started to read the first one when my cell phone rang. It was Christopher Marks.

"Any news?" he asked. "I assumed you just arrived."

"Yes. I'm at the host hotel, no news yet. I'll keep you informed."

"Christ," he said. "This is killing me."

"Please try and relax," I said. "I promise I'll keep in touch."

If I had a dime for every time I've had this conversation

I glanced up and saw Dane Marks entering the hotel.

"He's here," I said, totally shocked.

"Dane is there?" Christopher yelled in jubilation on the other end of the line. I could hear him talking to somebody. His wife.

"He's alive," he kept saying. "Praise God. Matt, please. Don't let our son die." His voice came out in staccato sobs.

"I won't," I said. "Gotta go."

He was still jabbering in my ear when I ended the call and scanned the three emails Dane had received. All three were from Thomas Conrad. The guy was nervous as a circus flea, asking Dane to rendezvous with him in some gay bar in Miami.

I watched Dane now, shouldering his way through the crowd to the check-in desk. I switched off the computer, stuffed it in my bag and followed him. He was wearing jeans and a black, stretchy T-shirt. He looked hot.

*Why does such a sexy man want to die?*

My cell phone rang again. Annoyed, I took the call, keeping an eye on my target. One of my biggest pet peeves was traumatized clients calling constantly for updates. Sometimes they called at the most inopportune times.

About to rip Christopher a new one, I was surprised to hear Looky's slurred speech on the other end of the line.

"Sooooo." He dragged the word out. "I didn't know you'd developed a taste for old man cock. You know I've got a big one, and I've always thought you needed a damned hard fucking, Matty."

I was so shocked I couldn't respond for a moment. What the hell was he talking about? Then I realized he meant my client. He must have thought Christopher was my new man. What the fuck ever.

"Get lost, Looky." I hung up on him. As I neared the reception desk, somebody jolted me, and I banged right into Dane, who was busy arguing with the clerk about credentials. Dane turned and stared at me.

"I'm sorry," I said. "Didn't mean to rub up against you."

He gave me a disarming smile. "No problem." He turned back to the clerk. "Are you sure there's no credential with my name on it? Danny Dark."

"Positive." She shook her head.

Even from where I stood I could see the desperation, the hurt, the lost look in his eyes.

"I'm a nominee," he said, sounding embarrassed.

Now I felt dreadful for the guy. People were pushing and shoving, and he simply gave up. I saw him shoot to the left and make a beeline for the cocktail bars. I was right behind him. He had his cell phone to his ear, and I could hear him muttering, "Come on, come on," as he brushed past the crowd of people swarming in both directions. He changed direction, going from one entrance to another.

We traded glances. He looked surprised to see me again, ducked his head and shoved his way to a large, black leather lounge chair in the more elegant of the two bars. I hung back and watched his agitated conversation with somebody on the other end of the cell phone. I didn't think he'd stay long in his chair. I waited and was rewarded with his abrupt departure for the poolside bar outside.

The colorful guests for the evening's activities had spilled outside. This crowd seemed to enjoy showing off as much of their bodies as they could, but Dane Marks had one objective in mind by the looks of things.

Getting hammered. He took a seat under the faux-thatched roof of the bar.

"Greyhound, please."

Vodka and grapefruit. It was one way to get a required food group into your system I suppose. I sat a few stools away from him and ordered coffee.

Dane was staring deeply into his cell phone as if willing it to do something except just sit there. He suddenly flicked a glance up at me, but I've been a student of body language a long time and glanced away at the bartender, watching him pour my coffee into a tall glass.

"If you have milk instead of cream, that would be great," I said. My stomach rumbled, and I tried to remember when I'd last eaten. I thought it had to have been at least two days. I'd fallen asleep on the flight here and therefore missed the opportunity to purchase one of the airline's expensive boxes of crappy meals.

I sipped the coffee. It was great.

"Is that your stomach rumbling?" a voice asked. I looked across the small distance between me and Dane. He grinned at me.

I shrugged. "I guess it is."

There was always danger in communicating with your quarry. On the other hand, this was a different sort of case. Communication might be key. My only hope was that his father didn't suddenly call during our discussion.

"Long flight and I didn't eat," I said. Dane looked bored. He was flicking through his cell phone again.

"We've got some appetizers you can order," the bartender said. "Maybe you want some eggs?" He slid a bowl of peanuts toward me.

"Sure," I said because Dane was looking up at me now.

"Eggs sound good," he said. He ordered a second cocktail, and we both ordered scrambled eggs and toast. I pretended to be fascinated with my coffee when Dane leaned over and extended his hand.

"Danny Dark."

"Matt . . . Killian." We shook. I always hesitated giving my full name to a target in case they recognized it. Who the hell was I kidding? I wasn't Mike Hammer. I was just a beat-up, former LAPD detective trying to make a living.

Trying to give a suicidal man the will to live.

It was a tall order.

"Any relation to Adam Killian?" Dane asked. It didn't surprise me he'd introduced himself with his porn name. Probably everyone here did. I should have had a porn name.

"No." I grinned. Adam Killian was a damned hot gay porn superstar. I'd known him from the gym, but I wasn't his type. He liked bodybuilders. I liked closeted, dark and dreamy cops.

"Good. I hate him." Dane slugged down some more of his drink.

I was a little surprised.

"Great body. Not a care in the fucking world. Couldn't get him for one of my movies." Man, he sounded bitter.

"You're a performer?" I feigned ignorance.

"Are you fucking kidding me?" He shook his head. "You think I could do porn?"

I looked at him. "Sure. Why not? You're a good-looking guy."

"I'm a director."

"Sorry." This wasn't going well. He was belligerent.

Looking for a fight. Geez. He was just like Looky. Without eye makeup.

Our food arrived, and I was relieved to have something else to divert my attention. Of course, my cell phone rang. I glanced at the readout.

*Christopher Marks.*

Of course it was.

I let it go to voice mail.

"So where do you fit in?" Dane suddenly asked, his tone friendlier.

I didn't want to say I was a fan. He'd probably sneer at me.

"Actually," I said, "I'm looking to invest in movies."

A spark of interest, immediately tamped by his grumpiness.

I felt stupid when he didn't respond and even more ridiculous for having said anything at all. Like I said, I'd had no game plan. What had I been thinking? Fly to Miami and win him over, instilling in him the will to live? Igniting hope?

What was it his father had said? *I want him to know that love isn't just for sale. Love is all there is. He can find it. I just want him to hang on.*

*Stupid, stupid, stupid.*

"What's your genre?" he asked, forking eggs into his mouth. The question surprised me. I had a shot here. A small, open window. I had to say the right thing.

"I like hardcore sex. But I'm interested in something artistic."

Dane looked at me and laughed. It was a hollow, horrid laugh. "Dream on, cowboy." He glanced at the bartender. "Get me another greyhound, will you?"

He was now on his third drink that I knew of. God knew how many drinks he'd had on the flight coming over here, but I could already tell he wasn't a happy drunk. He reminded me more and more of Looky. No. My mother. She was the type who looked at a hole in the ground and wondered, *can I get out if I go down* and went down anyway expecting to get stuck. She'd once described to me that this was her take on life. Life was like a manhole. It stunk of shit, but it was shit she could deal with. It was what she faced climbing out of the hole that frightened her.

"You don't like art?" I finally asked Dane.

He grinned. An actual, genuine grin.

"I'm a director. I love art."

"Do you steal?" I asked.

He stared at me. "What did you say?"

"I asked if you stole. I read a quote from Quentin Tarantino, who said—"

"Yeah, I know what he said. It's one of my favorite quotes. He said all directors steal. They don't do homages."

I grinned. I knew it was one of his favorite quotes. I'd found it on his laptop. I was swimming in safer waters now.

"Do you feel that way about your own work?" I asked, biting into the most fragrant, delicious, rosemary infused bread I'd ever eaten in my whole life.

"I do. I mean, I . . . did."

My mouth stopped moving of its own accord. The breath stuck in my throat.

"You . . . did?"

"Yeah." He bit into his own hunk of bread, nodding approvingly. "I guess I've given up on porn."

"Arty porn doesn't sell?"

"It sells but it doesn't pay. Big difference." He signaled the waiter for the check, quickly forking his eggs down his throat. He flicked a glance at the tab when the bartender slid him the small plastic tray.

Before I could do anything, he'd broken off a few twenties, dropped them on the plate and gave me a fake salute.

"Good luck with your investments, cowboy."

And with that, he was gone.

I pondered my next move once I'd paid up and decamped from the bar. I didn't want to make contact again, not after such a bad exchange. I reflected on what I'd learned. Not much really, except that I did wonder what Dane Marks was like when he was sober and not planning to end his life with one big party.

Strolling casually along the tables dotted poolside, I noticed Dane ordering yet another drink from a waitress carrying a laden tray. I sat several tables away where I could keep my eye on him, but he'd have to turn all the way around in his seat to get a glimpse of me. The festivities in and around the pool were turning a lot more adult than a few stray honeymooning couples would have liked. Nude couples swam and sunbathed without any embarrassment.

I overheard one young woman complaining to the waitress that she felt like she was "on the set of a porno. This is not what I want to see on my honeymoon!" I noticed Dane getting up and speaking to her.

"You want to swap hotel rooms with us?" the young woman squawked. Dane's voice was low, but the young bride was loud enough that I got the gist of the conversation. They all went inside, the waitress scurrying behind with her tray.

"Do you want to pay for all the drinks now or do you want me them charge it to your room?" she called out.

"I'm a friend of the groom's," I lied smoothly waylaying her. "Maybe I can take care of the check as a gift. I grabbed it off her tray before she could stop me. I scanned the paper quickly and saw Room 3215 scrawled in the corner.

"Oh, wow." I handed it back. "Sorry. Bit rich for my blood." I dropped it back on the tray. Eighty-seven dollars. What the hell had the honeymooners been eating and drinking that cost so much?

The waitress narrowed her eyes at me as I ducked inside the hotel lobby. I spotted Dane and the unhappy couple at check-in.

"Are you going to comp our champagne for our time, emotional duress and our trouble?" the bride asked loudly as I got closer. Ah, champagne. That explained the tab.

"No, I'm sorry. We've given you two free bottles already," the patient desk clerk responded. "We explained when you booked that there would be an adult awards convention at the hotel over the next few days."

"Yes, but when you said adult, I assumed you meant straight. Why would I want to be around a bunch of faggots on my honeymoon?"

Dane's head turned, and he stared at her.

"Jeez, babe," the groom said. "You just had to go there, didn't you?"

"Most of my friends are gay." The bride put a slim hand on Dane's shoulder. "But I don't want them on my first vacation as a married woman."

Dane muttered something. I watched him negotiating with the clerk and the newlyweds. I was so worried her outburst would mean that Dane would reject the room, but I realized the clerk was willing to work with them all.

"I'm getting packed," the bride trilled. "Lucky you." She leered at Dane. "We didn't even try out the bed yet!"

With a sigh of relief, I retreated to one of the comfortable lobby chairs. I watched Dane texting with admirable speed on his cell phone. The concierge brought him his suitcase, which he'd evidently left with the hotel staff. A bellhop grabbed the bag, Dane not even acknowledging the guy, and walked toward the bank of elevators. I waited a beat until I could hear several pings.

I approached the front desk. The clerk smiled at me.

"Good morning," I said. "I'm a late arrival. Last minute attendee. I know there's probably no chance but have there been any cancellations on rooms?"

"I'll no more in a couple of hours," she said. "If you want to check in with me at eleven o'clock, I may be able to help you."

"Thanks. I appreciate it."

"Why don't you give me your cell phone number. Will you be attending any of the events here?"

"Yes." I still couldn't get over it already being nine o'clock. I gave her my contact details."

"Killian," she said, frowning. "Oh, wait. Are you any relation to the other Killian?"

Before I could respond, she tapped away at the computer keyboard with rigid candy apple red nails.

"Adam," I said, hazarding a guess that perhaps he'd cancelled.

She beamed at me. "He kept his room reservation even though he won't be using it. Apparently his flight was over-booked back in LA and he won't be here until late this afternoon. He's coming only for the awards ceremony and taking the red-eye out again tonight."

"Oh, I'm sorry to hear that. I was looking forward to seeing him."

"He said the rest of the party would be checking in. Are you one of his go-go dancers?" she asked.

*Go-go dancers*? I stared at her.

"He wasn't sure if there were three or four dancers arriving," she said. "The room is available right now if you'd like to freshen up."

"Great," I said. She asked me for a credit card to "hold the reservation" which I knew was hotel speak for "we need a card so that we can bill all your calls and booze in case you decide to give us the slip."

I handed over my overburdened black Amex. Twenty-four hours ago I was feeling sorry for myself and my unpopular life. Now I was posing as a go-go dancer. I could do it for a few hours. I could take a shower, rest up, drink some coffee, spy on Dane's email messages. I could give the other dancers who showed up the slip before anyone figured out I was an impostor.

She gave me the keycard to my room.

"Will you be needing help with your suitcase, Mr. Killian?" she asked.

"No. I'm fine, thanks."

I smiled and took off for the elevators. I was in room 3222. Not far from Dane's new room. I saw the newlyweds swan out of the elevator in a cloud of obnoxious perfume, trailed by more luggage than any two people would ever need on a romantic vacation and stepped inside.

"Sheesh," what is that?" asked a woman as she stepped in beside me. She frowned. "Is that fly spray?"

"It does smell like it," I agreed.

She sniffed suspiciously at me.

"It's not me," I said, trying not to feel offended.

"Oh, it was bridezilla, was it?"

The elevator filled quickly. Everyone complained about the perfume until somebody farted, giving everyone new reasons to whine.

I was almost sick to my stomach by the time I got to my floor. I'd held my breath most of the way and released it as I charged along the corridor. I could smell cigarettes and pot and something else. It was strange and yet familiar. A metallic, chemical smell. Oh crap, someone was cooking crystal meth in their room.

At my door, I slid the key card into the slot across the top of the door handle. The green light flashed, and I opened the door. It was a very nice room. Two double beds. No champagne, unlike the bridal suite, but it would do. I immediately closed the door, set up the computer on a round table overlooking the balcony and, beyond it, the hotel environs hugging Miami's South Beach bay.

I checked Dane's messages online. He'd alerted his two rent boys that there was a change in location. He told Thomas Conrad and Ricky Stanton that he was staying at the Hyatt. He left his cell phone number and signed off with DD.

Danny Dark.

I realized now that the name suited him. He was a dark personality. Or rather, that side of his personality was strong. I hoped it wouldn't take over completely. I called his dad next and woke him. He seemed relieved when I told him I'd checked into a room on the same floor as his son.

"How much is that costing me?" he asked.

"Nothing. I'm posing as a go-go dancer. Somebody else booked the room."

"A go-go dancer?" He laughed so hard I found it frankly offensive. It wasn't that funny.

"Don't call his room," I warned Christopher. "I don't want to spook him."

"I won't. I'll be good. I promise. Go-go boy. Ha! I made a funny. Go boy! Go-go boy! Ha ha!"

"I'll be in touch," I said and ended the call. I took a quick shower, dried off, and threw on fresh underpants and a T-shirt. I checked the computer again and found that Dane hadn't had any responses to his text messages. Perhaps his rental boys were mid-air or something. I turned off his computer and tucked it into my bag, putting it beside the bed. I was trashed. Absolutely exhausted. I set my cell phone for a two-hour nap. I'd be no good to Dane or his father unless I got some rest. I slid between what felt like expensive bed sheets, my body caving in to sleep.

It wasn't long before I was awakened however and the

sensation was bizarre. It felt like somebody was sucking my cock. Wow. Talk about wet dreams. I tried turning over, but another man's body had me pinned to the bed. I lifted my head a little and glanced down.

*Holy fucking fuck fuck fuck.*

I was getting a monster job, and it was no dream. I was poised between Heaven and hell. On the cusp of screaming "What the fuck do you think you're doing?" and gripping the man's head to me in case he tried to stop.

But he wasn't stopping.

*Fuck . . .*

I looked down at the totally astonishing sight of my target, Danny Dark, AKA Dane Marks, sucking my cock.

As if his very life depended on it.

# CHAPTER FOUR

Dane knew what he was doing. For a moment, I just watched through half-closed eyes, enjoying the vision of his tongue swirling around and around my cockhead. I recognized the technique. It was a patented blowjob element typical of a Danny Dark movie. He'd shot one movie for his company in a circus setting, with all the sideshow freaks and weirdoes getting it on with unsuspecting patrons.

It was one of my favorite movies to be honest, though I wasn't sure what it said about me that I enjoyed the half-man, half-woman getting it on with an assortment of men he/she insisted should wear stockings and stilettos that he/she tore apart with his/her teeth.

Dane seemed to enjoy giving head as much as I enjoyed getting it. He was fully clothed, his eyes sparkling dangerously.

*Stoned.* His pupils were like pinpricks in his haunting blue eyes. I could have stared into them forever except that he had just sucked my cock all the way into his mouth and down his throat. The euphoric expression on his face only heightened my erotic high. He closed his eyes, and I watched as his eyelashes kissed the faint dusting of freckles on his cheekbones.

He worked my cock better than anyone I'd ever encountered in my personal life or ever seen on screen. He released me, much to my anguish, but I almost shouted out with joy when he began tonguing my balls. He pulled on the ball sac, tugging with his lips. Another patented Danny Dark maneuver.

I liked it. His fingers curled underneath my tightening sac to dig into strategic places. I jumped. He grinned up at me around a mouthful of my tender sac skin. Nobody had ever done to me what he was doing. His middle and forefinger dug up into what felt like a vein. He pressed. The charge of electricity that shot through me felt like such high voltage I was surprised my feet weren't puffing out smoke.

He moved his fingers a fraction more. Another press. Another high-wattage sensation. He'd found a meridian along the sac that was so intense it was almost unbearable.

"Huh," he said, releasing my balls and swallowing my cock again. His fingers dug deep into my sac again, and I came with a roar. The pleasure-pain was mind-blowing. I didn't think I would stop coming. He stayed on me, swallowing like a champ.

I slumped against the pillows, still in shock that he kept me in his mouth, long after my rage of fire had abated. He tenderly took his mouth from me, licking at my juices. He flicked his tongue across my balls, smiling.

"Thanks," he said when he finally released me. "That was on my bucket list."

I was totally taken aback. I had to fight my way out of the gorgeous fog he'd infused in my brain. "A blow job was on your bucket list?"

He grinned and slapped my thigh. "No, idiot. Seducing a sexy stranger. Why didn't you tell me you were one of Adam's dancers?"

"I—" I looked beyond him to a hulking figure leaning against the bureau. It was Thomas Conrad, otherwise known as the recently retired gay porn star, Tommy Terrell.

"Danny, if you've finished sucking the chrome off his tailpipe, we've got to get a move on." Thomas, looking feral yet hot with his new long, shaggy hair, scruffy three-day

growth and wearing jeans, white T-shirt and a Harley Da-
vidson leather jacket, was in a foul mood.

"Somebody shouldn't have jacked himself up on 'roids
the second he arrived," Dane purred, winking at me.

"I'm buildin' muscle. I've got a competition in three
weeks, ya know."

"Yeah. How could I forget?" Dane got off the bed and
moved easily over to Thomas, trying to wriggle into his
arms. Thomas clearly wasn't in the mood and tried to resist
as his cell phone rang. I recognized the tune and couldn't
place it for a moment. Oh, yes I could. Adele's *Skyfall*. Boy
was that a prophetic song choice.

Thomas frowned, muttering into his phone as Danny
snuggled into him, kissing the man's stern face. As a gay,
bottoming porn star, Tommy Terrell's biggest draw had
been his big, muscular build, but soft, handsome face. He
had been a novelty draw paired oddly with twinks with big
boners and a few famous, aggressive tops. In his new carna-
tion, he'd developed a hardness, a glassy frosting over his
good looks.

Ah yes, he'd become an angry, disillusioned young man.
Porn hardened people. Maybe it was a good thing he got out
when he did. I flicked a gaze at Danny Dark, AKA little lost
Dane Marks. I watched the way Dane kept trying to get
Thomas' attention. It was sad. Pathetic.

"We're not on the clock yet," Thomas grumped. It was a
shocking thing to say, and I saw the pain flooding Dane's
face. He looked wounded as Thomas pushed himself away
from him and kept talking into his phone about some movie
deal back in LA.

I pulled up my underpants and got off the bed. When
Dane's hurt gaze caught mine, I gave him a smile.

"That was the best blow job I ever had and the nicest
wakeup call in history," I said, kissing his cheek. He opened

his mouth to speak, and from the mean little glint I saw in his baby blues, I just knew it was going to be something vicious so I cut him off with a kiss on his mouth.

He seemed shocked but recovered quickly. "Ah . . . thanks." His face reddened.

"What's your name again?" he asked.

"Matt. Matt Killian."

"I remembered the last name. Not the first." He glanced down my body. "Where's your costume? Did Adam give you one yet?"

"Um . . . no."

"You make your first appearance in an hour." He sounded exasperated. "You wearing leather or lace?"

*Leather or lace?* Was he fucking kidding me? He moved over to a suitcase propped up on the table I'd been working on earlier. Thank God I'd had the foresight to pack away the laptop before I'd conked out. That would have given a whole new meaning to *awkward*. How would I ever explain why I had his laptop?

Dane opened the bulging suitcase and began pulling out stuff. I gasped. I'd never seen such tiny undergarments.

"You're very well endowed," he said, holding up a black leather jock strap, the cock mound covered in crystals that now cast off colorful glints around the room.

"I am?" I was mortified. I could never go out in public wearing something like that. My God . . . I couldn't even remember having donned such a skimpy garment for a lover in the privacy of a bedroom.

"This will look perfect on you. You'll fill it out nicely." He cupped my cock, making me jolt. "Yes, I think you will. Try it on, sweet cheeks."

He handed it to me. I had no idea how to wear one of these things. God, I was lamest gay man in history.

I gulped and took hold of the strap. My gaze fell on a pair

of black leather shorts that laced up on the sides, sitting on top of the pile in the suitcase.

"Wait. I want to wear those." Yeah, that was the ticket. More coverage.

He held up the shorts. "These? Are you sure?"

I almost screamed when I realized the front had been cut out. My entire cock and balls and what I'd eaten for the last three days would be on display.

"Er . . . no, on second thoughts, this is fine."

He put his hands on his hips. "Let's get a look at them then."

"These are heavy." The leather strap studded in so many crystals really was.

"Yes, I know. Adam has a thing for Swarovski. We'll have to bury him wearing his collection one day since he refuses to believe he can't take it with him."

He dropped the shorts back in the suitcase. Thomas finished his call and began pawing through the suitcase.

Dane reached over to me and began pulling down my underpants. I kicked them off, glancing over at Thomas, who'd shrugged off his jacket and was folding it up neatly over a chair, along with the rest of his clothes.

*Fuck me.* He had a monster cock. It had been one of his big attractions as a bottom, and he went commando. I watched him slide on the jock strap, and I followed suit. Hot dog. The leather pouch settled over my cock and balls and my body kind of got a swagger to it.

"You're a hairy one, aren't you?" Dane asked, running his hands over my body.

Thomas packed his meat into his own leather jock that had a gigantic arrow made of crystals pointing down on the front. He cast a practiced glance over me.

"I like the natural look," he said. He frowned slightly. "You aren't Adam's usual go-go dancer."

"Is that a bad thing?" I asked. If this guy figured out I wasn't really a dancer he was big and strong enough to hurl me through the triple-layer windows of the hotel room to a certain death.

"Naw. Just sayin'. Keep your dick on."

Dane laughed. "You both look so hot." He ran his palms over our bodies. Thomas was now lighting up a joint. So much for his text saying he didn't do drugs.

He took a deep hit and passed it to Dane, who took a quick toke. He held it out to me, and I shook my head.

"Sure?"

"Yep, I'm sure."

He shrugged and handed it back to Thomas. Suddenly he clutched the suitcase.

"Whoa! What the fuck is in that? My fucking head is spinning."

Thomas grinned. "Gift from a fan. A little formaldehyde."

*Holy fuck.* I was glad I'd declined.

"I can't eat for another three weeks, and it works." Thomas grinned. "Works like speed, and speed is good."

*You fucking nutcase.* I watched Dane reach for the joint again, and he took a deep hit. I winced inwardly. I was so thankful to be here. I had to keep my eye on the guy. He'd been drinking, and now he was smoking what we LAPD cops knew on the streets as a candy cane. It was a dangerous drug, and it worried the crap out of me that Dane just kept sucking on that joint.

"My head is spinning." Dane bent down, grabbing his knees. I rubbed comforting circles on his back.

"You okay?" I asked.

He didn't say anything for a moment, but when he straightened, I could tell he was ripped to the gills.

"Fine. Wow. I'm fine. You should try it. It packs a punch."

"No thanks. I don't like candy canes."

"Is that what they're called?" Dane took another hit and passed the joint back to Thomas who finished it off, using a pair of tweezers as a roach.

I was beginning to really hate the guy.

Dane got to my crotch. "I do think you fill this out so well." He batted his eyelids at me. Man, he was stoned.

"Thanks," I said. My cell phone rang and I moved to the bedside table. Holy fucking fuckity fuck. I should have known it would be Christopher Marks. I was feeling a serious case of contact high and grabbed the phone, smiling loopily at the two men in the room.

"Gonna take a leak, and this call." I shut myself up in the bathroom.

"What's happening?" Christopher squeaked in my ear.

"I'm with him," I hissed.

"You're with him? So he's alive? He's okay?" His sob sobered me up quickly. Dane's parents were frantic with worry and, yes, I was keeping an eye on their son, up close and personal, but they had to stop calling me.

"Yes, he is." I kept my voice low. "You have to stop calling me. I promise you I will get him home, but it won't be today. There are these awards on tonight. I mentioned those to you."

"Okay." I could hear Christopher talking in the background to his wife.

"I'll call you in three hours with an update. Please don't call and blow my cover, okay?"

"Okay," Christopher said again. I could hear Mrs. Marks saying something about her son being diabetic and was he taking his insulin. Insulin? It was the first time anybody had mentioned it to me.

"He takes pills," Christopher said. "He really needs them."

I rolled my eyes. "I'll get back to you." I ended the call as the door handle rattled. Then came a knock. I flushed the toilet and opened the door.

Dane stood there, grinning. "You're the shyest go-go dancer I ever met," he said, unbuttoning his fly. He stood over the toilet bowl, unleashing a very handsome cock. His death would definitely be a serious waste of manly assets.

"I guess." I shrugged. I was beginning to worry now because I could see the room filling up and dancers were squeezing their way into provocative outfits. Well, scraps of outfits. One guy wore leather chaps with his ass fully exposed. Another one grabbed the shorts I'd declined, and soon, they were drinking champagne. I allowed myself a glass. It helped blunt the shock of the news that I'd have to walk around the hotel in this outfit. No outer garments, no . . . nothing.

Grabbing my bag from the floor, I stuffed my cell phone and discarded clothes into it. A few of the models were trying to figure out the combination for the room's safe.

"I'll take everyone's belongings down to the concierge" Danny called out. Just give everything to me. We're headin' downstairs in fifteen minutes."

He took possession of everything and we all relaxed until Thomas handed around another joint. The effects were immediate. Two tweaked twinks began fighting over a pair of tiny black shorts with the zipper in back, I hoped we wouldn't have a girl fight before we got downstairs.

"There's only one outfit left," Thomas announced, reaching into the suitcase for a black leather thing that turned out to be a gladiator kilt with matching body harness. He claimed it before I could snap it up.

"Oh," he said. "This is *so* me." He peeled off his tiny jocks, tossing them toward the fractious twinks. He slipped on the kilt and harness, glancing over at me.

"Help me, will you?"

I crossed the small space between us and realized he was having trouble with the body straps. I loosened the fastenings, and then Dane was back in the room. Between us, we got that thing onto Thomas's body until it looked the leather had been molded to his sculptured form. We took a step back, and a kind of hush fell over the room.

Oh, wow. He looked amazing. It was as though we'd stepped back in time to ancient Rome. He really filled the outfit well.

"Fuck, babe," Dane said. "It's perfect."

I nodded. Thomas grinned as the guys swarmed him. He was enjoying himself now. He gave us each a good luck kiss and even fondled my ass cheeks. That was the first time I actually realized I was bare-assed.

He led the way, Dane following up behind. We left the room and piled into two elevators. On the ground floor, hotel guests swirled as we paraded past them. We got wolf whistles and a few gropes. One guy's hand slid into the crotch of my jockstrap, shocking me. I felt something papery as we proceeded. A twenty dollar bill. For doing absolutely nothing.

Boy was I in the wrong line of work.

I followed the herd into the ballroom where cameras popped, and I noticed the other dancers mingling with the mostly male guests, shimmying up and down on guys' laps, allowing them to kiss and suck their nipples, fingers, lips . . . I noticed money slipping down crotches, and I watched as Dane took photos. His camera focused on me as Thomas Conrad made a beeline for me. He shocked me by suddenly grabbing and kissing me, his hand shooting into my crotch strap.

It wasn't as much fun as it probably looked. He'd inadvertently grabbed some pubic hairs, and it hurt like hell as they broke off. His hand dug down deeper to grab my cock.

I was stunned when he pulled my cock out, holding it toward the camera, smiling.

I thanked God as cameras flashed and some idiot videographer asked me for my name, that nobody I cared about would be seeing the results of this fiasco anytime soon.

"Matt," I said.

"Matt what?"

"Matt Watt. That's it. W-a-t-t."

"Plenty of voltage and high watts. I like it." The guy leaned in and stroked my cock head. Thomas still held me in a painful grip. He was talking to some twink dressed in nothing but a pastie of a blue cupcake over his genitals.

I gently nudged Thomas and moved his hand from my cock. Dane waved to us, beckoning for me and Thomas to follow him. Somebody gripped my ass and, to my horror, I felt them spreading my cheeks. Thomas laughed.

"We get 'em all here," he said in my ear. I felt something hard poking at my asshole and jumped.

"It's only money," Thomas said, his lips touching my ear.

We followed Dane up the stairs. I copied the others, waving and blowing kisses to the crowd. Music started pumping, lights swirling around the room like some crazy big lava lamp and we moved to the back of the stage standing in line.

A huge drum beat and a black curtain dropped in front of us. I could hear a woman talking into a mike at the front of the stage, welcoming everyone to the pre-show. She whipped everyone into applause and, as we waited, I noticed the dancers pulling out their cash and counting it. I pulled the note wedged from my ass cheeks. A one hundred dollar bill. Between that and everything else stuffed in my crotch, I'd just made two hundred and seventy dollars. I rolled it all up and shoved it into my crotch again.

"There's a small seam sewn into the front to keep it secure," the twink beside me said. He reached in and showed me. "Adam is so clever about this stuff." He smiled when I thanked him. The money and my crotch felt a lot more comfortable after that.

The MC announced that we'd be doing a couple of numbers for the crowd's entertainment. Dane flew up and down the line.

"Do you all remember the routine?"

*Routine?* What routine? The curtains started to rise.

"Shake those tushies!" he trilled and scuttled off the stage. Bright white lights threatened to blind me from the foot of the stage. From a crappy sound system somewhere, *Party Like a Rock Star* blared. My teeth formed themselves into a petrified grin as the crowd screamed and the other dancers all formed an apparently well-rehearsed line.

All except Thomas Conrad who stepped right in front of me and began to showboat, strutting, gyrating in a rhythmless way, thrusting his groin up provocatively with every bizarre dance step he took. It was so insane, he threw every dancer beside me off, especially when he began doing high kicks.

Personally, his was a brilliant maneuver from my point of view. I could hide behind him, and nobody would see that I didn't know a single step.

The other dancers, however, were furious and started competing with him for attention. The music morphed into the ultimate gay strip club anthem, *Relax*, and my inner gogo boy came out, and I started doing my own thing as the others did, too. A series of Perspex boxes rose from the stage floor in a lilac haze of dry ice smoke. I tried to hop onto the nearest box in a frenzy of disco heated applause. I felt a pair of hands hoisting me up and looked down to see Thomas Conrad grinning up at me.

No longer worried about having to match the other dancers' movements, I threw myself into the moment and enjoyed myself dancing like a fool. The crowd loved it. As the song wound down, the boxes slowly descended back to the stage floor, and I grimaced as I was once again forced to dance, messing up the whole routine. The MC returned to the stage, and the black curtain fell in front of us as we took our bows.

"Thomas, you ass!" a couple of the guys hissed. "You weren't supposed to be up here!"

"Yeah!" chorused a grumpy Dane as he strode toward us. "You threw poor Matt right off his game!"

"Ah, bullshit!" Thomas yelled over a fresh flood of music. "The little whores out there loved it!"

"Well there's no time now and, you!" Dane pointed at Thomas. "Stay away from Matt for the next number."

"I don't mind. The crowd loved him," I insisted.

"Sweetie, the crowd loves anything we give them." Dane turned on his heel. "It's the Goldfinger number next, girls!" he yelled over his shoulder.

I had no idea what the hell the Goldfinger number was, but I was pretty certain I'd screw that one up, too.

Backstage, a couple of twinks in matching A & F shirts and artfully torn jeans handed out pairs of tiny and tight shorts made of gold tissue lamé, which we were urged to carefully pull up over our leather jocks. Next, we donned spray-painted gold work boots that were not very comfortable on our bare feet, but the go-go dancers seemed oblivious.

"Five minutes, ladies! If you need the john, go now!" Dane instructed. I noticed he had a digital camera and snapped photos here and there. I dashed off to the restroom only to find Thomas Conrad sitting on the toilet seat injecting something right into his cock.

"What the hell is that?" I asked as somebody else turned up beside me.

"Apomorphine," the voice beside me said. Dane.

I turned to look at him.

"They used to give this to gay men in drug tests back in the fifties to try and cure their homosexuality," he said. His eyes looked empty and dark. "They even tried it with me."

"I thought they used it for Parkinson's," I responded. Now I had him talking about drugs I wanted to keep the conversation going. How could I introduce the subject of his insulin?

"That, too." Dane gave me an appreciative look, then glanced at Thomas. "How long will that keep you hard?"

"Couple of hours. I got the sex show on stage then a hot date with you." He winced as he withdrew the needle. "That shit hurts, man."

"I could never shoot up myself." Dane shuddered.

"Lucky you don't have to take insulin," I said.

His face contorted. "I know, right?"

Thomas was laughing as he rubbed his cock between his palms. It was so flaccid I wondered how he was going to get through a live sex set.

"What's so funny?" I asked.

"Oh . . . I was with my dad recently, and he caught me taking a pill." Dane gestured toward Thomas. "We had dinner with him, and when my dad asked me about it, Thomas lied and said it was insulin."

"What was it?" I asked.

"Dilaudid."

*Street heroin.* I knew enough about Looky's addictions in the past to know that Dilaudid had a strange effect on people. Yes, it induced euphoria, but it had a catastrophic downside; suicidal tendencies and delusions.

"Are you still on it?" I asked, recalling the summer when I was seventeen, and my mom and I staged an intervention on Looky. It had been a painful excursion into the world of drugs and delusion. It had cost my mom her entire life savings to get Looky into the Betty Ford Clinic. Sixty-five thousand dollars for one month's stay. He'd booked after two weeks and vanished into the Mojave Desert.

When he came back to the family house a few weeks later, he found that my mother had cut him off from all contact and his kids were perfectly content in my care. He was a crazy-maker, and our peaceful existence was short-lived. With him was Ellie, the woman who was to become the bane of my teenage years. The woman he'd met in rehab and discovered a love for all things chemical. My dear stepmama. That's how Looky saw her anyway. One more person to help him with his kids. One big, happy, fucked-up family. I stared at Dane.

"I like it," Dane said, looking stubborn and defensive. "But I like other things, too."

"My stepfather used to take it," I said. *True.* "It made him suicidal. He tried to take his own life several times. *Not true. Looky's too narcissistic to even dream of harming himself.*

Dane gave me an odd look. "Really?" He chewed his bottom lip. His cell phone rang, and he pulled it out of his back pocket, rolling his eyes as he checked the readout. He shook his head. He was about to say something, but Thomas cut him off.

"My dick hurts like a motherfucker."

"It does look swollen," I said, "but not in a good way."

In fact, his member looked lopsided and purple, with strange welts materializing over it.

"Holy fuck," he said, his face turning people. "I think I injected the wrong stuff into it." Sweat poured down his face.

"What did you shoot into it?" I asked as Thomas began to heave.

"Coke," he rasped. "Liquid coke and PCP."

*Holy shit.* I'd heard about this latest street craze. What did the kids call it? A Doubleheader. "Give me that." I yanked the cell phone out of Dane's hands and called 911.

"I'm okay," Thomas gasped, his whole body shaking. His cock looked like it had gone ten rounds with Mike Tyson.

"Get an ice pack from housekeeping," I told Dane, who nodded and took off as I helped Thomas out of the crapper. He let out a blood-curdling scream, and a couple of twinks came running.

"Help me," I implored as I tried to lower the big slab of muscle to the floor. He was in so much pain, one of his balls taking on a distended shape that had one of the twinks running from us. The other one helped me.

"I'm a trained nurse," he told me as the 911 dispatcher put me on fucking hold. Was she kidding me with this? "But I've never seen anything like this."

Thomas shook and shuddered under us, his body feeling beyond hot and sweaty. The operator came back on the line, and I explained our problem.

"He's a performer," I said, "he injected an enhancement into his penis and—"

"An enhancement?"

"He injected what he thought was Apomorphine, but he now says it was a mixture of coke and PCP."

"A ride or die?" the operator sounded shocked. "I'll have a crew out there immediately. Stay with me, Matt."

The next few minutes were a maddening blur. Thank God for Dane and the twink nurse who kept cool heads as the other dancers flocked around us.

"What's happening?" the operator asked me.

"I need air," I shouted. "Move back, people."

Dane stood and pressed the onlookers back. Hotel security arrived, and the two goombah-looking guys had no reaction as they gazed down at the trembling, frightened model thrashing on the floor.

"Help me," Thomas said, gripping my hand. "I don't want to fucking die!"

"You're not going to die," I assured him, but the truth was, I had no idea if he would. I had no clue how much and exactly what he'd been ingesting all day.

The operator kept asking me what else he'd taken. I mentioned the laced joint. I told her he'd also used steroids.

"Ask him if he took GBH," she said.

I repeated the question to Thomas.

"Sure I did," he said. "Mother's milk."

*What?* What the fuck did he say?

He cracked a smile at me, his face a terrible mask of pain as the paramedics arrived and took over. Dane and I stepped away.

"So that's what it looks like," Dane whispered, looking down at his friend on the floor.

"What?" I asked.

"Letting go."

"That isn't letting go," I said. "It's a death dance. It's a man's agony as he fights for his life."

"Fuck," Dane said and brushed past a couple of twinks in his rush to get out of the room.

# CHAPTER FIVE

I couldn't find Dane anywhere. I hurtled down the service stairs and back through the reception rooms as the 911 operator kept talking in my ear. I'd forgotten she was there for a moment.

"You need to go back," she urged. "The patient is freaking out."

Torn between following Dane and doing the right thing, I chose the latter and finally understood the age-old adage that sometimes doing the right thing was the hardest.

Thomas had been hauled onto a gurney and was wheezing into an oxygen mask.

"You want to come to the hospital?" one of the paramedics asked as Thomas gripped my fingers with his sweaty paw.

"Not like this."

"Get changed and meet us at the service entrance," the paramedic said. I nodded and took off for the front desk. I was shocked when several hands reached into my gold shorts shoving more money into them. I tried to twist myself out of the way as I ran across the ballroom. I heard the MC announcing the award for best director of the year. It wasn't Danny Dark.

Oh, boy. I grabbed an elevator and found myself posing for photos with a couple of guys who insisted they were my biggest fans.

"I've seen all your movies!" one said.

"Would you like a threesome with us?" the other guy

asked. "And what do you charge?"

"I don't swing," I shouted as the doors pinged open. I ran for the concierge desk and asked for my bag. The concierge wanted proof it was mine when I pointed to my small suitcase once she unlocked the huge storage space.

"My laptop's in there and my jeans. A T-shirt. My wallet and cell phone."

She glanced at my hand. "I have two phones."

The 911 operator had ended our call, and the cell phone was ringing. Christopher Marks. I took the call.

"This isn't a good time," I barked into the phone. "I'll get back to you."

"Is my son all right? Why are you on his phone?"

"An accident backstage. I'll get back with you."

The concierge opened my bag, and when she saw I'd been telling the truth, she let me take it. I could tell by the look in her eyes that she expected a tip. I dipped into my crotch and pulled out a slightly moist bill. A twenty.

Dammit! A whole twenty bucks!

I handed it to her, almost laughing at the horrified expression on her face.

"It's either that or two singles in my wallet." I shrugged.

"This is fine," she said smoothly, pocketing my twenty. She pointed the way to the men's room at the side of the lobby, and I ran into a stall and changed. I now had Dane's cell phone and laptop but had no idea where he was. I ripped off the stupid gear I'd been strutting, dropping them on the floor. Money fell everywhere, and I picked up the notes, shoving them into my bag as I threw on my street clothes, shoving my feet into my running shoes. I left the sparkly stuff and took off for the lobby, about to ask somebody where the service entrance was.

To my immense relief, I spotted Dane at the elevators. I shouldered my bag and went to him, pulling at his sleeve.

"There you are," I said. He looked at me, his bewildered gaze finally registering who I was.

"Didn't recognize you with your clothes on," he cracked, though his face looked ashen. He seemed very upset. "I didn't win anything. Not that I thought I would. I couldn't believe I was even up for best screenplay. Mind you, it would have been nice to win for that. They were the best twelve pages I ever wrote in my life."

Twelve pages? Hollywood screenplays were typically a hundred and twenty pages though for a porn movie, twelve pages must have seemed like slogging through *War and Peace* for his models.

"We have to go to the hospital with Thomas." I tugged him toward me as the elevator pinged.

He shook his head. "I'm not going anywhere. I've got to find my cell phone."

"Here." I shoved it into his hands and dragged him with me past reception. "Where'd you find it?" he asked, looking puzzled.

The concierge stopped us.

"The ambulance is gone," she said. "Your friend is on his way to the Jackson Memorial Hospital. I've arranged to have one of our airport shuttles take you there."

"Thank you," I told her. Dane reluctantly accompanied me, and we hurtled into the van awaiting us.

"I so don't want to do this." He slouched into the bench seat beside me as the van sped off.

"Don't like hospitals?" I asked. *Because from the sounds of things you've been spending a heck of a lot of time in 'em lately . . .*

He shrugged, wrapping his arms around his body. The scowl on his face had been patented by teenagers eons before.

I didn't say another word, wondering if he would. We rode in silence for several blocks. He finally said, "I really hoped I would win. I know it's stupid. But I thought if I win . . . just once, if I could win something before I die I'd — "

"You're planning to die?" I asked, trying to make it sound as if I were joking. I caught the van driver's gaze in the rear-view mirror and looked away.

"I was planning a . . . farewell party tonight." Dane's words came out in a whisper. I booked two escorts. Got me some drugs and I was planning to go out with a bang."

"Two escorts?"

He shook his head. "Thomas was one of them. Man, he told me he didn't take drugs. He gave me some green powder to snort, and it's made me feel like shit."

"We'll have the hospital staff take a look at you."

"No, we won't."

"Yes, we will."

We arrived at the entrance, and I was certain he'd run from me as soon as he could. I held onto the bottom of his T-shirt and dragged him into the emergency doors.

After checking in with the duty nurse as her name tag called her, she told us to take a seat. Whatever Dane had been taking had started to take effect. He began to shake and retch. A few people sitting around us in the waiting room moved away. I approached the nurse again.

"I've been watching him," she muttered. "What's he on? Bath salts?"

"Bath salts! I'd never take bath salts!" Dane huffed. Yeah, and wasn't it Whitney Houston who'd once said "crack is whack?"

"Don't let them take me," he said, gripping my arm. "I've had two hospitalizations. I can't take it anymore."

I stared into his eyes and took his hands in mine. "Can you let them check you over? I'm worried about what you've been taking."

"Don't leave me," he said, a single tear running down his face. "If they lock me up . . ."

"I won't," I promised. I accompanied him to a curtained cubicle where he peed into a plastic bottle, and the nurse put it into a contraption that would give them a snap analysis of what he'd been taking. Urine test. I'd seen similar things in emergency rooms. As she played good nurse, another played bad nurse and came in to ask Dane for his insurance card. Surprisingly he had one.

He became nervous as she took his ID and insurance details and left the cubical. Good nurse informed us that they wanted to check what drugs he'd been taking.

"Our intern will be with you shortly." She shot him a worried look.

He lay on a hospital bed, eyes closed. I sat beside him on a hard plastic chair, and we waited.

"You know," he said, finally, "I've tried to kill myself a few times and it never works. Something always happens. This time, I thought my plan was foolproof. I paid two guys who know how to have a good time, and I planned to party with 'em, then send them on their way and finish things once and for all with a shed load of drugs."

Neither of us said anything for a moment. He shifted on the bed and looked at me. "I tried before. Booked a couple of guys, one of them seemed to actually like me. And it wasn't just because I was paying him. He came back because he was suspicious. He called security. I was pissed as hell at the time. I guess now I should be grateful."

"I think it would be a sincere waste for you to leave this life," I said. I leaned across the bed and kissed him. He was so surprised at first, he lay rigid, then began to respond.

The curtain rolled back, and a harried-looking young doctor in a lab coat that looked way too big for his slim frame said, "We need to talk. You've got seven different pharmaceuticals running through your system. I'm surprised you haven't had a heart attack."

Within seconds, his cubicle became the scene of total chaos. Orderlies shifted in machines to monitor his vital functions. Nurses stripped off his street clothes, and I took possession of his cell phone once more, and his wallet. The hospital staff worked so quickly I became alarmed. Two of the nurses moved up and down his body, placing electrodes all over him. Another drew blood as the harried doctor lectured him on the stupidity of consuming designer drugs whose origins emerged from the cupboard underneath his kitchen sink.

It was obvious as the machines began to run that his heartbeat was racing and his blood pressure had soared sky high.

"Am I going to die?" Dane asked, his eyes enormous blue puddles of terror.

"No, but you could have a stroke and wind up in a world of hurt. You've got cleaning chemicals running through your bloodstream," the doctor said, his tone severe. "Look at this." He tapped the monitor that showed Dane's accelerated blood pressure rate. One more pill and you could wind up a drooling vegetable. Is that what you want?"

"N-no, not at all." Dane had turned chalk white as the nurses tried feeding a tube into his mouth.

"No, no! Not again!" He screwed up his eyes, gearing up for a tantrum.

"We're going to have to pump out your stomach," the doctor insisted. Dane thrashed and yelled, but to no avail. He looked petrified as needles went into his arms and the pumping tube made its way down his throat.

I stepped out of the way. The original nurse I'd seen at the admissions desk tapped my shoulder. She beckoned me, so I picked up my bag and leaned over the bed. Dane's gaze collided with mine.

"I'll be right here," I said, trying to keep my tone soothing. "I need to check on Thomas."

He shook his head vehemently and began to retch.

"I'm right here. I promise." I stepped outside the curtains and followed the nurse.

"Your friend is in very bad shape," she said. "We've resuscitated him twice, and he's on a respirator. We've made contact with his wife, and she's on her way here. Just thought you'd like an update."

"He's *married*?" The gay porn industry would never cease to amaze me.

"Yes." The nurse gave me a funny look. "I don't think she's very happy with him. He told her he was going fishing with his brother."

I had to fight the urge to laugh. She shook her head at me, giving me an ironic half smile. I turned to head back to Dane's room when his cell phone rang. It was Christopher Marks. With a loud sigh, I walked outside and took the call.

"How is my son?" he asked when he heard my voice.

"Getting his stomach pumped. I don't want to lie to you."

"He overdosed?"

"Not really. He's been partying pretty heavily but I'm with him, and I think he's going to be okay. I'll stay with him, I promise."

"What about his insulin?"

I hesitated. "He isn't diabetic," I said. The silence on the other end of the phone was deafening.

"That's not a huge surprise, but a tremendous disappointment." Christopher's voice seemed to break with emotion.

"Look, I'm going to stay with him. I'll talk to him and see what he wants to do from here, but I have to tell you, he was pretty frightened when he realized he might now die but become permanently impaired."

"That's good, I guess, but I'm really pissed at my son.

We've been frantic over his diabetes." He took a deep breath. "Text me with updates. I'm so upset right now I'm likely to tell him to fuck off and never call me again."

"You don't mean that."

He paused. "No. You're right. I don't. But you don't know what it's like wondering each time the phone rings if it's going to be some hospital telling you that your son is gone."

*I have some idea . . .*

"Matt, I'm sorry. You've been great. Actually, Stu Gressing told me your stepfather's an addict. That's kinda one of the reasons I thought you'd understand about my son."

"I do understand, sir. And anger is a healthy emotion. It's important to own it. Addicts have a way of making us love them and also wanting to beat the heck out of them. I'll keep in touch."

As I ended the call, I walked back into the hospital. I wondered if I'd saved Dane Marks's life and figured I pretty much had. If I hadn't dragged him here, he would have stayed at the hotel and partied on.

Back at his cubicle, he was lying in the fetal position, gagging and retching, I could smell the strong odor of salt and bile. Tears flowed down his cheeks.

The nurse helping him gave me a sad smile.

"If you want to rub his back that will help distract him," she said. I felt so bad for Dane as she finished the purging. "A gastric lavage is no fun. You're doing great." She smiled down at Dane, whose body seemed so fragile as I rubbed his back and shoulders.

I've never liked the smell of vomit and have always found that a mere whiff of somebody else's puke makes me want to yodel groceries. I turned my face away to get my bearings. I waited until the nurse had removed the tube from his stomach and wiped away the goo from his mouth and hands and began rubbing his shoulders again.

He didn't speak for a long time, maybe twenty minutes. He kept dry heaving, and when he did finally speak, his voice was hoarse.

"That was horrible."

"I'm sorry."

"Don't be. It's not your fault. Jesus, I feel like shit." He turned his head slightly. "You saved my life."

I squeezed his shoulder, and he leaned into me.

"Thank you."

"My pleasure."

"You've seen me at my worst," he rasped. "And you're still here."

I squeezed his shoulder again. "Just relax."

"Relax? I need to shit my brains out now." He sprang off the bed and took off running. I followed him, but he really did need to go to the men's room.

As I waited outside, I saw a thin woman in the scrap of a red dress running into the ward. I gaped at her. I recognized her from numerous run-ins with the paparazzi back in LA. She was a well-known transgendered TV reality star.

"I'm looking for my husband," I heard her saying. I wasn't surprised when she yelled out Thomas's name followed by a lusty, "I'm so gonna kick your ass, Tommy!"

Sometimes, being single didn't seem so bad . . .

Dane was released four hours later to my custody. The only reason he wasn't committed to a seventy-two hours hold was because his overdose hadn't been intentional. We returned to the hotel, where the concierge held his belongings. He seemed subdued and ashen-faced.

"I keep thinking about Erik Rhodes. He was one of my closest friends in the business," he said when the taxi dropped us off at the hotel. "I used to counsel him about all the reasons he shouldn't die. He was a hella nice guy, no matter what the fuckin' bloggers said. When he died, I didn't really see a reason to hang around anymore."

"Were you lovers?"

He shook his head. "We talked about working together. We used to encourage each other. We were working on a screenplay together, but he really had a death wish."

I took a deep breath. "Do you?"

He hesitated as we stood outside the revolving glass doors. "No, I guess I don't. I just want the pain to stop. I want to believe there's something more. I used to love this business, but I see so many of my friends dying. I'm sick of being hurt. I'm an artist, and this business chews us up big time."

Inside the hotel, he retrieved his bags. It was now seven o'clock, and the awards were still going on. We glimpsed inside the open doors of the ballroom and saw that there was a wild *Kinbaku* rope-tying session taking place on stage. I glimpsed a couple of well-known BDSM performers up there, but bondage and tying are not my thing.

"I'm glad they're calling it by its correct name," Dane whispered to me, pointing to the large sign outside the ball-room. "So many Doms call it *Shibari,* which is the wrong word. We westerners fuck up everything, don't we?"

"Yes, we do." We smiled at each other. "How are you feeling, Dane?"

He blinked. "How do you know my real name?"

"I've just been at the hospital with you."

"Oh, right. I think I need a nap. I need a nap and a quiet room." He passed his hand across his eyes. "I've book a suite over at the Mandarin Oriental. I don't suppose you'd like to come and hang out with me."

"I'd love it."

Outside, we grabbed a taxi and headed to the hotel, which seemed a world away from the gay porn awards as we peeled across the Brickell Bay Bridge. The oceanside city shone like a million prisms, a rainbow-kaleidoscope of colors reflected in the water. The hotel rose like a star-spangled phoenix on the shores of Brickell Key.

From the moment we stepped inside, our feet sinking into the luxurious carpeting, I felt Dane relaxing and, therefore, so did I. We checked in, the manager giving us an "oh, you're gay" look before granting us the keycards to the suite Dane had booked. We rode the elevator to the fourteenth floor. The place was so tranquil I wondered if we were the only guests.

Dane swiped his card, and the door eerily swung open on its own. Inside, we both stared at the sumptuous surroundings. It sure beat the Motel 6 I'd stayed in on my last case.

"Wow," Dane said as he inspected the wraparound balcony with a view of the ocean and the downtown skyline.

I was so mesmerized by the enormous welcome basket, I couldn't think about much else. Would it be rude to sample some bread and cheese?

Dane turned around and saw that I was studying the edible gifts so tantalizingly out of my reach.

"Help yourself," he said. "Let's eat. I'd kill for a beer." He moved over to the fridge and caught my eye as he opened the door. It was well stocked, but I didn't think a beer was a great idea. "Don't look at me in that tone of voice." He grinned. "All right, all right, I'll have mineral water."

He grabbed a bottle and flopped on the bed. "Come and sit with me." He opened the cap and extended a hand to me. I grabbed an apple and moved beside him. He swigged straight from the bottle.

"Ah . . . that's better." He grinned, put the bottle on the nightstand and scooted closer to me, putting his head on my lap. I inched back a little on the bedclothes and shoved a couple of pillows behind my back. He settled, getting more comfortable. I stroked his face and neck, brushing his hair back with gentle fingers.

"God, I must smell," he said, bolting up. "Come and take a shower with me."

Boy, he was all over the place, but a shower did sound good. He didn't smell so great. We kicked off our clothes and, with reluctance, I left the apple on the nightstand. He opened his suitcase and retrieved a Louis Vuitton toiletry bag. I almost fell over when I saw the volume of contents when he opened it in the bathroom. He traveled with more lotions and potions than any woman I knew.

"How does this smell?" He held a bottle to my nose, and I detected good things like sandalwood and jasmine.

"Very nice."

"Edible," he said, wiggling his eyebrows. I'd just realized he was naked and he looked really . . . edible. I had qualms about us getting naked and soapy-wet. He was a fragile guy, and I had been hired to find him. Okay, I'd found him. He was alive and, judging by the reaction of a certain part of his anatomy, damned happy.

He turned on the shower taps, and water came out from three different showerheads. Of course, once we submerged ourselves and his hands and mouth were all over me, I no longer had any doubts I was doing the right thing.

Heck, his dad might even give me a tip for making his son so . . . delirious. Dane squeezed the body shampoo over both of us, and we began to rub up and down each other. He got to his knees and began to suck my cock. I wanted to tell him to stop, but it felt too good and, man, he looked so beautiful doing it.

I stroked back his hair. His blue eyes opened briefly under the warm, scented spray. He sucked me deeply, his mouth tight around my shaft. Fuck, he knew what he was doing. I couldn't resist, especially when his hands moved to my ass cheeks to hold me closer. He pressed his fingers into my butt, massaging me. Oh, God. I wasn't going to last.

When I came, he released me, grinning as he swallowed. One good turn deserves another.

"Fuck me," he suddenly said.

I bent and took his hefty cock into my mouth. He'd said the shower gel was edible and he hadn't been kidding. It tasted like fruit and nuts. I almost went crazy from the combination of scents and flavors. I sucked on him as he gently humped my face. I held his solid hips and worked him relentlessly.

"Don't," he suddenly said. "I want to come with your cock in my ass." He pulled out of me and turned, offering me his ass.

"Need rubbers," I said, wild with desire for him. I stroked his crack. I longed to fuck him.

"You sure?" he asked, a wistful tone to his voice. He might have been flirting with the idea of disaster, but I wasn't. "In my bag on the vanity," he rasped. "Hurry."

I stepped out of the shower. My brain kept hammering at me not to do this, but I wanted him. And he wanted me. I stepped back in, Dane bouncing on his toes. I bent and kissed his ass cheek, about to delve for more.

"Fuck that, stick it in. Hurry." He wagged his butt in my face, and I quickly rolled on the rubber. He braced himself against the pristine white wall tiles and pushed his ass out to me. I ran my cock up and down his crack, groaning when I reached his hole. He pushed back against me, and I began to slowly enter him. I felt as if I'd entered a hot oven, yet the sensation was blissful. Warm, wet velvet entrapping me. I fucked him faster and harder now, reaching around his hip to grab his cock in my hand.

"Oh, yeah. Fuck. Amazing!" He grinned at me over his shoulder, and I dropped a kiss on his lips. They tasted salty from the stomach pumping, but his skin smelled like fruit. Forbidden fruit. His cell phone was ringing, but we were too far gone.

I fucked him until we came within seconds of one another. He collapsed against my chest, and I kissed his shoulder, my cock still thundering inside him.

Getting cleaned up wasn't much fun. I longed for a rematch, then swiftly felt guilty that we'd fooled around at all. We turned off the taps, toweling off. We brushed our teeth and got into bed. I was about to say I didn't think we should play anymore, but it was hard to resist a man feeding me bread and brie and succulent red grapes with his fingers. We ate until we couldn't swallow another bite.

His cell phone began to ring again. He leaned over and picked up the phone.

"Ricky Stanton," he said aloud.

My heart almost stopped. He was the second model Dane had booked to party with him . . . one last time.

"Hey," Dane said, taking the call. His face turned red, and he gave me a funny look.

"Yeah, um . . . look, I've met someone, and I kinda want to hang out with him." He paused, and I could hear Ricky's agitated boom on the other end of the line. "Hey," Dane interrupted him, "I paid you. Consider it a gift. Drugs? No." He shot me a worried look. "Do whatever you want with them. Sorry, Ricky."

He ended the call. I wondered what I should say. In the end, I thought ignorance was bliss.

"Boyfriend?" I asked.

"No. A trick. I told you I booked a couple of models to play with but—"

I flipped him onto his back and started kissing him. His cock grew hard at my touch.

"You know," he said, "I love the feel of your skin. Say,

you ever tried erotic body painting?"

"Can't say I have."

"There's a place we need to try in SoBe. It's called Skin. A friend of mine just opened it." He reached across the bed for the landline. When the operator called, he asked for a limousine to take us to South Beach."

"A limo?" I asked as he hung up the phone. "Isn't that a little extravagant?"

"It comes with the room. We also get complimentary spa service. Come on, let's get changed."

He bounced out of bed. Man, did he ever sit still?

I followed him, throwing on fresh jeans and a T-shirt and my running shoes. We dressed hurriedly, running downstairs to find the limo waiting. We made out in the backseat, my hands fumbling in his fly for his cock.

When we got to Skin, I didn't know what to expect, but the place was jumping. Dane held my hand and booked us a room. I was surprised it was dark inside, a bouncy mattress and an array of body paints in the middle of it. The walls and ceiling had been painted dark blur with pin-pricks of starry lights.

Once again we threw off our clothes. We crawled across the airbed, which was a couple of feet tall and the size of a double king-size bed. We knelt, facing each other. He smeared gold paint on me. It felt smooth and cool on my skin. He went on and on, painting me gold, stopping to lick my cock head. He smeared red and blue stripes along my arms, then I started painting him.

Our breathing grew ragged.

"Huh," he said as we started rolling around on the mattress. "How thoughtful of them to put a couple rubbers in the toy box."

I lay between his parted thighs, feeling like an ancient sun god about to take the man he'd conquered.

Dane held me with his legs and arms, so tight it was hard to get room to slide on the condom and work my way inside him.

His fingers clenched in my hair, our mouths meeting in a frenzied kiss. I could smell paint, flowers and stars spun in my eyes as I entered him hard and deep.

Dane's tongue probed mine. I let him pull and push, feeling as if I was riding a deep ocean wave, waiting for the water to wash over us.

He came between our heated bodies, his eruption igniting my own.

"Fuck," he whispered into my mouth. "Holy fucking fuck."

# CHAPTER SIX

Dane loved the nightlife. We went from one disco to the next, one gay club, then another. Interestingly, like me, he liked to hang back and watch.

"I'm a student of human nature," he said. "I take it all in." He seemed to be happy enough with plain mineral water until we walked into one club where the drink du jour was a Shirley Temple. We ordered one each, laughing and drinking the virgin mix until we had an attack of laughter that sent us back to the hotel.

"I can get us a private car on my Uber," he said.

"Your what?"

"Uber. It's a special app for a private car service. You press some numbers and hey, presto."

We found a taxi right outside. We climbed in, Dane lying down with his head in my lap.

Finally, the frenetic watcher of people was still.

I took the opportunity to text Christopher Marks.

*Dane is fine. I'm with him, and we've spent the evening togeth-er. He seems to be doing great. I won't be charging you anymore for my work. I'll send you a final invoice upon my return to LA. Will advise you as soon as I know when this will be.*

"Who are you texting?" Dane asked, opening his eyes and looking up at me.

"A client." Oops . . . I hadn't meant to say that.

"You're a businessman, right? What kind of business? Oh, wait. You said you make investments. How did you get into go-go dancing?"

I laughed. "I didn't."

He sat up then. "What do you mean?"

"I kinda got dragged into it."

"Really? Is that why your dancing was so awful?"

I winced. "Yeah. That'd be why."

He grinned at me. "We can't all be dancing queens." He leaned back against the seat twisting his body around the other way, throwing his legs over my lap. I slung an arm across them.

The cab driver stopped. "I gotta go slow here. People are dancing in the street." He grinned. "Saturday night in SoBe."

It was a far cry from LA. Even our certified gay city of West Hollywood wasn't like this on a Saturday night unless Mardi Gras was involved.

"We're in no hurry," Dane said, leaning back against the seat. I tried to identify the many scents in the cab. We'd showered off at the paint place with an apple-cherry soap, and I could smell carpet shampoo, too.

I wondered how Angus was doing with my cat and put in a quick call to his cell phone.

"Who you calling now?" Dane asked in a sleepy, playful tone.

"My brother. He's looking after my cat." I got Angus's voice mail so I left him a message.

"You have a cat? What kind is he?" Dane seemed fully alert now.

"A Maine Coon."

"Is he sweet?"

"No. And I think he hates me. He sprays everything and thinks he's boss."

"You're lucky to have a cat." His face fell. "I lost mine a couple of weeks ago." His features twisted with grief. "I keep hoping she's okay and that nobody hurt her. She's the sweetest thing. What happens to all the pets that

84

disappear?"

I shook my head. "I don't know."

He closed his eyes, and I hugged his ankles.

"I'm sorry about your cat, Dane. I really am."

"I have this secret fantasy she'll come home. What's your cat's name."

"Ronin."

"Oh, well, now see, there's your problem. You've named him the masterless samurai. You'll never be able to tell him what to do."

He fell silent for a moment.

"What's your cat's name?" I asked.

"Her name is Stardust. Because she's a sexy cat. I swear she was Betty Boop in another life."

"That's a great name for a cat. I kinda have a funny feeling you'll find her again."

"Thanks for saying that."

He turned his head as we started inching along the bridge back to the hotel.

"Are you hungry? The Mary Brickell Village is right here. We could get something to eat, then go back to the room."

"Sounds good to me." I leaned forward and asked the driver to stop.

"Now you tell me. And I'm stuck."

"Sorry." I gave him a decent tip, and we piled out of the cab. Another couple grabbed it and I saw his face brighten.

"Good things happen when you're around," Dane said. "Come on, I know a really cool little place here."

He took my hand, and we darted between throngs of entwined couples, both gay and straight. He lost his way a couple of times but finally found Le Boudoir Brickell, an intimate French restaurant with a pink interior and a pervading smell that had me salivating.

"They have this sandwich that is unbelievable. Will you

share one with me as an appetizer?" Dane asked. He seemed so excited to be here that I had to say yes. I perused the menu and swallowed. Hard. It all looked so inviting.

"I really want a glass of wine," he said, glancing at me.

With my hard stare on his face, he soon shook his head. "I'm not an addict. I'm more of a . . . dipsomaniac. When I drink or pop a pill, I go to excess. I will have a Shirley Temple, though."

We ordered the mystery sandwich he pointed to on the menu, and we both wanted the Churrasco steak with blue cheese sauce and French fries.

The sandwich arrived, and I might just dream about that thing until the day I die. A warm ham and cheese sandwich on soft, lightly toasted bread, we dipped in béchamel sauce that was so divine we finished it off with our spoons. The steaks were amazing, and I even liked the grilled asparagus Dane had ordered, though frankly, I am a meat and potatoes man. I can live without vegetables.

Not that I said so. We ordered espressos as we finished our meals and my cell phone rang.

Angus.

"Mind if I take it? I want to check on my kitty."

Dane smiled. "Of course not."

Angus sounded surly. "Ronin peed on the bed in the middle of the night because I wouldn't get up and feed him. He's the most antisocial cat I've ever met in my life. When you comin' home?"

"He's never peed on the bed before," I lied.

I caught Dane's grin. "Well, maybe once," I admitted.

"This cat thinks he's a fucking pasha," Angus said. "Just like Dad." he hung up on me.

"Trouble in paradise?" Dane smirked. I told him all about Ronin. It was hard explaining my life with Looky. And suddenly I realized I was telling him more than I told most people.

He knew who Looky was and seemed surprised he was still living in LA.

"I thought he'd be enjoying his post-rock career living on some vineyard up in the Napa Valley."

"The closest he'd get to a vineyard is cheap wine at Trader Joe's," I said.

"You know what's funny?" He leaned back against his chair. "I went to a party at his house once. Maybe twelve years ago. No. More. He had this amazing place up on Wonderland, and I found out later it had been the site of some really gruesome murders."

"Was it a Christmas party?" I asked.

Dane looked at me. "Yeah, come to think of it, it was."

"Was there an elephant in the living room?"

He blinked, then began to laugh. "Yes. Wait a second. This rings a bell. It was the back half of an elephant in blue . . . cement I think it was. I didn't take it in at first. It was a fireplace mantel. Strangest thing I've ever seen."

"My mother made it."

"Oh, sorry."

"No, no, don't be. I love elephants, but that thing was hideous. It was her Christmas present to him, and I was there. I was at that party. I was the guy hiding in my room, lying on my bed reading *Spiderman* comics."

I was aware of my face falling. *Spiderman*. I still had no idea who'd busted into my office and relieved me of many of my most treasured possessions.

"You read Spidey?" He shook his head. "Love Spidey. Which is your favorite comic?"

We talked about that for several minutes, neither of us quite able to believe we could have met eons ago.

I skirted around the issue of why I'd come to Miami, even though he asked. I changed the subject, tactfully I thought, asking about his porn career. He seemed to be honest when he told me about his life and how hard he'd found it to get work outside of the business.

"I've been tarred with a very unforgiving brush," he said. "If it's this hard for me to get back into mainstream work, I can't imagine what it's like for the performers. Guys don't last as long now as they used to. With the Internet, there's no hiding. No freedom, no privacy. I know one very talented model who even got chucked out of art school because he did gay porn."

"That's not fair."

"No, it's not. And I've tried so hard to go straight, as it were. I've resorted to answering ads on Craigslist. You know, there are some real freaks out there. One guy wanted me to stand in a corner of his living room while he modeled these weird uniforms and he wanted me to pencil-sketch replicas for him. I did them of course, but it was really uncomfortable. He paid me by check. Of course, it bounced. I saw those sketches online recently. He sold them all to a major designer. Wonder what he got for them . . ."

When the check came, Dane picked it up. I begged him to let me pay. His father had told me he was in debt and I didn't want him to do more damage to his credit card. We argued a little more over the check. I won.

On our walk back to the hotel, we held hands. I felt on top of the world except that I was hiding a huge, terrible secret. I wanted to tell him the truth, but I couldn't. I genuinely liked this man, and I wanted the chance to see if we could make this work.

We stopped outside the building, swapping hot kisses.

"I'm so glad I met you," he said, squeezing my fingers in his. "I really feel tonight like . . . like I'm not so alone anymore." He blushed. It was so cute. "Sorry. I sound like an idiot."

"No. You don't. I'm glad I met you, too."

"You know how you told me this morning that you were interested in investing in a gay porn movie?"

"Wow, was that this morning? So much has happened since then." I shook my head. "But yeah, I remember."

"Don't do it. Please don't. I'm going to get out of the biz, and you shouldn't get into it. It's a trap. A seductive trap but all it brings is sadness. I told my dad the other day that this business taught me that love is for sale."

"No, Dane. Lust is for sale."

"See what I mean? It screws up your thoughts. When we get back to LA, I'm going to start going to AA, and I'm really going to put some thought into an entirely new line of work."

"That sounds good to me."

"And I hope we can keep seeing each other."

"That sounds especially good to me."

He laughed then, the first serious belly laugh since I'd met him. We went to the room, cleaned our teeth and fell into bed. Though our cocks were hard for one another and the flesh was definitely willing, our minds and spirits were a different story. I fell asleep with Dane in my arms, my hand curled around his cock. He said something, but I couldn't hear it and was in no shape to respond. I was worlds away dreaming of disco dancing, gold boots, and money. Lots and lots of money . . .

I awoke around six in the morning, which would have made it three o'clock in the morning back in LA. I'm an early riser by nature, but this was ridiculous. Something was wrong. My eyes opened, and I peered through the sleepy blur. Dane wasn't there. I struggled to rise and quickly scanned the room.

The bathroom door was closed. I bashed on it, but there

was no sound. I turned the handle. It gave. I pushed it open, so relieved to find it empty. I moved around the suite, but he was nowhere to be found. My bag was exactly where I'd left it, but I was worried that he'd taken off. Had he found his laptop in my bag? I quickly opened it. Nope, still buried under a pile of clothes. I grabbed all the money I'd made dancing and smoothed out the notes, putting them into my wallet. I zippered my bag up again.

When I saw his shoes on the floor, I relaxed. He was somewhere in the hotel.

I busied myself making coffee. They sure had a fancy setup that made me miss the one I'd just sprung for back home. I smiled thinking that with my dancing tips I could replace the coffee maker I'd lost. That got me thinking. Why hadn't Stu Gressing gotten back to me on the fingerprints I'd sent him. I checked my cell phone for messages and saw a text that had come in overnight.

*Call me. Surprising news on the prints. Hope all is well and swell.*

It was three o'clock in the morning in LA. I didn't think he'd appreciate a wakeup call. I'd just have to wait.

I realized I'd flown into town on a slightly more expensive ticket than normal. A flexi fare that would allow me to book a return flight at my convenience and without any extra charges. I made a mental checklist of my billing for Christopher Marks. I'd have to pay him back a sizeable chunk of his advance. Not that I cared. He had returned my text message saying he was happy to receive some money back.

The smell of brewing coffee persuaded my brain that my body no longer needed sleep. I poured myself a cup and was halfway through it when Dane returned.

"That's not how I wanted to find you," he said looking sexier than hell in his board shorts and a black T-shirt.

"How did you want to find me?" I looked up from my cell phone.

"Naked and in bed. Preferably hard. Waiting for me."

"Spoken like a true movie director. Any particular pose?"

"Yes, lying on your back, beckoning me for a kiss."

"Will this do for now? I mean I *am* naked, but sitting is sort of lying down, right?" I beckoned him, and he laughed, swinging down to kiss me.

"I went to the media center downstairs. They don't have free WiFi in the rooms, which I think is weird. Anyway, I couldn't change my ticket."

"You bought a return ticket?" I asked.

He gave me a severe look. "Of course I did. If you buy a one-way ticket in this country, they flag you at the airport as a possible terrorist."

"I read that somewhere, but I really didn't know if it was true."

"Yep. It's true, and my flight leaves at eleven."

"What airline?"

"American."

"I'm traveling with United."

"We still have time to get frisky and have a little fun." He wiggled his eyebrows. I finished booking my flight for twelve noon. I wasn't happy with my seating arrangement. I was stuck in the middle section in the middle seat. If I had children wedged on either side of me, my misery would be complete.

"What time do you leave?" he asked.

"Noon."

"We need to hurry. I want you to fuck me at least three times before we leave this room."

"What's checkout time?"

"We'll be gone before then." He checked his phone. "We have two hours. Let's get busy, gorgeous."

He jumped on the bed, and I jumped on him. I didn't mind being directed by him. I didn't mind at all.

I restrained myself from tearing his clothes off.

"You should know I want to get back early because there's a really cool AA meeting tonight. I already contacted my sponsor, and I'm—"

I silenced him with kisses. Then the thought occurred to me. "Dane, aren't you supposed to be single for the first year of sobriety?"

"Hell, no." He looked up at me, an indignant look on his face. "You are a big part of this. I want to spend some time with you. I want to see if we can work this out. You think you can deal with that?"

"Yeah," I said, kissing him fiercely. "I think I can cope." I bent my head and began kissing and licking my way down his body, loving the way he responded to everything I did. He was a fabulous lover, and it amazed me that his father didn't think he was handsome enough to be a porn star. Maybe his dad just hadn't *wanted* him to be a porn performer. Dane was more responsive than the guys he directed and, to me, a lot hotter.

When I reached his cock, I wondered if I could bring him the kind of sizzling magic he'd brought me when he sucked me off the day before.

His body arched in pleasure as I let my tongue roam his massive girth. He really had one of the meatiest, tastiest cocks I'd ever seen. It took some getting used to. I sucked him slowly but not gently. I took my time, savoring his glistening head. He pumped in and out of my mouth, clearly enjoying himself.

I took him in a little deeper. I'd never been a size queen, but now I openly lusted for his huge tool. I let my throat get used to him.

"Oh, yeah!" he shouted. I could tell he was beyond excited now and I worked hard to keep up with him. I sucked him harder and faster, loving the taste of his sweet juices against the back of my throat. I could taste blue cheese and ironically, 7-Up. I tasted it all.

I swallowed him as much as I could as his cock ruptured deep into my throat.

He sank against the bed. "Geez," he said. "Good morning!"

We made love nonstop, finally forcing ourselves to get out of bed and shower. We changed into jeans and T-shirts. I worried that he might be depressed going back home, but he seemed fine. We exchanged numbers. I gave him my cell phone and the house landline.

He didn't need my office number until I could explain things to him.

*Jee-zus. How the hell am I gonna do that? I'm not sure I can explain things to myself . . .*

We shared the limo to the airport.

"Would you like to come back here sometime?" he asked me, sounding suddenly shy.

"Sure," I said. "Only next time, I'd like to spend the whole day in bed." His face turned pink with pleasure. We dropped him off first, and it was hard to let him go. He came back to the limo twice to kiss me goodbye.

"Call me when you get home," he said on the third kiss. I promised I would. I was worried now. I had his laptop, and he'd look for it when he got home. As the limo pulled away, I called Christopher Marks. I got his voice mail, so I left a message telling him I needed to see him when I got back. I told him I had Dane's laptop and that I wanted to drop it off and also give him back most of his money.

He called me as I cleared the security checkpoint and I moved to the side to take the call.

"Am I to understand you've become friends with my son?" he asked.

"Yes, sir."

"He just called me from the plane. He's crazy about you. I

must say your methods are unorthodox, but I am just relieved to hear my son sound so happy. You woke him up, Matt. I don't know how I can ever thank you."

"Thank me by not telling him you hired me to find you. He's still . . . fragile. I don't want to hurt him. I really care about Dane, and I need to tell him in my own time."

"Okay," he said. "Look, I'm picking him up from the airport. He's going to have dinner with his mother and me. First time in weeks. That'll give you a chance to drop the laptop back at his apartment. You can give me the keys when we meet. Are you sure you don't want to keep the money I gave you?"

"Very sure. I'm just charging you for the airline ticket. Three hundred and twelve dollars."

"What about the hours you put in before?"

"I can't charge you for that. I feel very good about finding Dane and helping him."

"That's nice, but I want you to keep five hundred. You're a good man. An honest man. You can give me back the rest if you insist."

It was not until I got on the plane that Stu Gressing returned my call.

"You're not going to like this, but we did get a hit on the fingerprints in your office."

"Who was it?" I asked.

"Your mother."

"My . . . mother?"

"She's in custody at Santa Monica Jail. She got caught breaking into several offices in your building with some guy called Dave Findlay. You know him?"

"Yeah, I know him." I couldn't keep the venom out of my voice. "He was my dad's best friend. What the hell were they doing robbing everyone? I thought she was in India."

"She was. They're back. Ran out of money I guess."

"Oh, man, she could have asked me."

"Yeah. Woulda. Coulda. Shoulda. They can't make bail, and he's got three priors. You want to leave them in the joint?"

"Not much I can do from here. I'm in Miami."

"Gotcha," he said, ending our call.

I felt like a criminal sneaking into Dane's house and re-planting his laptop. I took a moment to absorb the silence. I stared at the empty cat dishes on the floor and suddenly missed Ronin tremendously. I drove home, pleased that the city had dried out. I wondered if Ronin had forgotten me and become attached to Angus, but when I walked in the door that crazy feline threw himself at me feet. I bent to pat his fluffy head as he rubbed his face against my shoes.

And then he bit me.

Yep, he loved me.

I shook my head and straightened. Angus wasn't home, but his stuff was piled high. I could detect the strong and unpleasant odor of eau de cat piss as I shut the door. I put my bag on a chair and looked around. It had only been two days since I'd been here, but it seemed longer.

Ronin meowed loudly and huffed his way into the kitch-en. I meekly followed. I wasn't sure if he'd been fed because he wolfed down food faster than a feral mountain lion so I opened a fresh can of Fancy Feast just to be polite. Ronin loved the fish varieties, but his stomach could only tolerate chicken so I always prettied it up with torn shreds of plain chicken. I opened the fridge. His chicken was gone, which meant Angus had eaten it and I'd have to get more.

I stared down at the cat, who glowered at me. Yep. He wanted his chicken.

"Be right back," I told him. He opened his mouth in what may have been his idea of a smile but to me looked like a threat of imminent danger.

I'd told Dane I'd call when I got in, so I sent him a text. I grabbed my car keys and cell phone and left again. I took a deep breath as I heard the cat throwing himself against the door. He'd hose everything in sight, just to retaliate, I was sure. I should have gone straight to get the chicken and returned to the apartment, but after picking up a few staples at Trader Joe's, I was restless. No response from Dane. I hoped that wasn't a bad sign. I fought off the urge to contact him again and got into my car, which seemed to have a mind of its own.

Before I knew it, I was on my way to Santa Monica Jail. I was going to see my mom.

There is an air of unreality to this particular jail. It is fairly new. A beige and grey concrete jungle tucked discretely away on Olympic Drive, it's as if the seaside city of Santa Monica can't quite believe it houses prison inmates. I almost laughed as I passed through the entrance marked with the words Santa Monica Public Safety Facility.

The words my mother and safe didn't belong together. And I was right. As I went inside, I learned she'd been released.

"Who bailed her out?" I asked the cop on duty. Officer Larrimer wasn't familiar to me, but then I didn't know a lot of the jailhouse staff since I was no longer a member of the LAPD.

"I know who you are," Officer Larrimer said as she checked my ID. "You were the motorcycle cop who got shot on the 405."

"Yeah." I took a deep breath. "That was me."

"You don't ride anymore?"

I shook my head. The nightmares of pulling over a suspect in a stolen vehicle and being shot at point-blank range had abated. But the *daymares*, as I called them, of people reminding me of my fall from grace didn't stop. Somebody always remembered me. Somebody always had an opinion. Most cops were cool. They understood it was hard to give up being a cop, especially when you've been forced to do it by some asshole with a gun.

"You look good for a guy who was forced out of work. I thought maybe you were a paraplegic or something."

"No. But I was—" Aw, geez, why did I have to keep explaining things. "Injured. Three weeks in the hospital. They gave me a handsome settlement. They wanted to get rid of me."

She stared at me.

I looked her in the eye and admitted the truth. *Finally*. I'd resisted saying it for so long because it hurt. It fucking hurt. The truth sucked.

"The guy I chased down on the freeway was a former cop. He stole a car and abducted his girlfriend's kid. The case was messy. Paying me off and getting me out of the way was . . . convenient."

"Yeah. I heard that. People say you got a bum deal. They thought you'd sue them."

"I waived my rights to a lawsuit." My voice cracked. I'd taken the advice of attorney who told me to make it all go away by accepting the money. I could start to heal. Get an actual life. I was now beginning to see that Christopher Marks wasn't wrong. Love *was* for sale. I'd loved being a cop. It was my whole world. And I'd allowed that love to be bought and paid for with a chunky check.

"She posted with Chewey's," Officer Larrimer said, bringing the conversation back to the business at hand.

"The bail bonds place?" That surprised me. What the hell kind of collateral had Mom posted with them?

"It was nice to meet you." She shook my hand. "Stay off

the freeway." She grinned.

*If I had a dime for every time, some asshole said that . . .*

I nodded and thanked her for her time. I drove over to Chewey's on Wilshire Boulevard and found Bill, the night desk guy, watching gay porn hidden in a straight porn case. I recognized the DVD as he let me in and I glimpsed the action on his laptop. A Danny Dark classic.

Bill and I went way back. We'd gone to the same high school, the same college and then our paths diverted when he went to prison for armed robbery, and I became a cop. He'd found God and boxing in the joint and had also been forced to give up his pugilistic passions when an MRI showed pinprick holes in his brain.

"How are ya, Matty? Say, we bailed out your old lady. Chewey did it as a favor, but she's gotta show up in court tomorrow at ten. She can't fuck it off like she did last time."

"Last time?" I gaped at him. "There was a last time?"

"Yeah. She shoplifted at Needless Markup."

That was the nickname for Neiman Marcus, and it shocked me to know my mom had been shoplifting.

"When was this?" He wheeled his chair over to a slightly bent looking filing cabinet. He pulled her file and thumbed through it.

"Two months ago. We managed to get mediation for that one, and she got community service."

Light was beginning to dawn . . .

"What kind of er, community service is she doing?"

"Battered women's shelter. She says she's been stealing stuff to make the women's lives better."

Yeah. And unfortunately for my mother, it was the sort of thing she would do.

"You got an address for her?"

"She's at the Gateway Motel on Twenty-first. Room number nine."

"I'll make sure she makes her court date."

"Swell." He jotted down the details, and I thanked him before pushing off again. Next, I went to see my mother, who opened her door only after I threatened to kick it in.

"Where's Dave?" I asked her.

"Still in jail."

"What the hell are you doing?" I exploded on her, making her back away.

"I don't need your help," she said, her tone icy. "You have money. Plenty of money. Those kids in the shelter don't have anything. They can't even buy a lollipop."

"So you thought you'd steal from me? Your son?"

"You always were so self-indulgent. All those comic books and the coffee maker. You . . . you . . . you're spoiled. That's what you are!"

"Spoiled! Are you kidding me? You fucking abandoned me!"

"Oh, here we go." She put a hand on her hip and rolled her eyes. My mind went blank, and I stopped caring. I stopped hating her, and I decided I wasn't going to worry about her anymore.

"Make the court date tomorrow or don't. And, by the way, I'm pressing charges. You had no right to steal from me. Breaking and entering is a crime. All I did was love you." I put the piece of paper with her court details on the table beside me.

"Love don't mean a thing," she said, her tone bored. "It don't cost a dime."

"That's where you're wrong, Mom. It costs . . . *everything*."

She frowned, not getting me. I wasn't sure I got me. I left the motel and drove home. My cell phone rang as I unlocked the door and Ronin whined at me.

"Hey," a voice said. Dane. "You busy?" he asked.

"Nope." I kicked the door shut and walked to the kitchen, the cat pawing at my ankles.

"Feel like company?"

"Well, I would except the place stinks. My cat's been spraying like crazy. You know what? I don't think I've even heard him purr. Ever."

"If you don't want to see me just say so." Dane sounded hurt.

"For God's sake, of course I want to see you. Get over here, will you? Just don't say I didn't warn you."

"Give me your address. I'm on my way."

# CHAPTER SEVEN

"Oh, my God, you weren't kidding. That smell is awful." Dane walked into my apartment and glanced down at the cat. He bent to scratch his head before I could warn him that Ronin was a biter.

"Did you make that smell?" he asked Ronin who flung himself on Dane's shoes. I felt a stab of wild jealousy when Ronin submitted to being picked up and cuddled and, fuck me. He was *purring*.

"I like what you've done with the place," Dane joked, pointing to the banked up towels and blankets at the windows.

"From the rain. I haven't been around to clean things up."

"Well," he said, "let's get started."

I tried to stop him, but he seemed bent on cleaning. Maybe this was a good thing.

"Where's the laundry room?" he asked. I pointed down the hall. Ronin went mad when his new best friend left him as he went back and forth with a stack of damp, smelly sheets and towels.

He followed Dane like a dog when Dane came back and began spraying the walls with the rubbing alcohol the vet had suggested. Ronin was all over Dane. I supposed that was better than attacking him, but when Dane looked in the fridge after getting the last load of laundry in the washing machine, he gave me a severe look.

"Is this how you live? Should we order out?"

I was about to say yes when Angus came home with a

girl. He seemed embarrassed to see me.

Angus, this is my friend Dane," I said. "Dane, this is my brother."

The two men shook hands. "This is Annie," Angus said. "Isn't she lovely?"

Annie leaned all over Angus.

"Adorable," agreed Dane.

"We were just going to order some food," I told Angus. You want to join us?"

"Are you back for the night?" He cut a glance toward the bedroom. "I was hoping to stay here another night."

"No problem," Dane said. "We can order some food and Matt can come stay with me tonight." He gave me a wicked grin. "Unless you prefer the sofa."

"No, I prefer to come home with you." I went through the collection of takeout menus. We all settled on Thai and Angus opened the fridge, looking for beer.

"All you've got is mineral water, apples, and that chicken," he complained.

"The chicken belongs to the cat," I told him.

"No beer?" He stared again as if a six-pack would miraculously appear.

A thought occurred to me. "Don't say anything to Dane about the computer," I whispered. "Please."

He straightened. "That's him? You found him!" He grinned at me.

"Don't say anything," I repeated.

"All right, all right. I heard you the first time." He slammed the fridge door, and it shook.

As the food arrived, I took care of the fluff and fold in the laundry room and returned in time to hear Dane sharing his plans to open a restaurant.

"A kind of art café," he announced. "We'll have resident models and art classes. Photography . . ." His eyes shone.

Both Angus and Annie seemed to be enthralled by the idea.

"What do you do now?" Annie asked him.

"Not much. I'm a graphic designer, but it's hard to get work these days."

She gave him a funny look. "I'm a model, and my agent says she can't find anyone to do her logos and brand imaging. Not that I really understand all of that. Maybe you could talk to her."

"Sure," Dane said. "Hey, who wants a Vietnamese spring roll?" He loaded up our plates, and I noticed Ronin sitting on the floor looking up at him.

"Finish your food in the kitchen," Dane told the cat. Ronin padded away, content as a clam.

"How'd you do that?" I asked.

We spent a fun hour dissecting our family lives, and it occurred to me that Christopher had told me Dane was going there for dinner. Had he had two meals or had something gone wrong?

As I came back with the last load of laundry, I heard him saying that he'd gone to visit his parents on his return from Miami and he'd had an argument with his dad.

"I argue with my dad all the time," Angus said, forking an asparagus spear.

"Me, too." Dane seemed to sag a little. "I had to go to an AA meeting, and they were upset that I wouldn't stay and have dinner."

"AA? You go to meetings?" Angus asked. "So do we. Which one do you go to?"

They began chatting about their favorite meetings, which turned out to be the same ones. As Ronin crawled into my new lover's lap, I felt alone again.

Naturally.

Angus and Annie made the bed and claimed it for their

own. Dane took charge of me and the cat and drove us over to his apartment.

"We're not leaving Ronin there. He hates it. He's a people pussy. He wants to be with us," Dane insisted.

I didn't argue. I was still in awe that Ronin hadn't sprayed anything for close to two hours now.

At Dane's apartment, the cat ran from room to room as if exploring his new digs. He seemed quite chipper about the whole thing. Dane opened up one of the cans we'd brought and fed the cat. By my estimation, Ronin had eaten about six already that day, but I didn't say anything.

Dane grabbed my hand. "As for you, I have something else in mind."

He dragged me down the hall to his bathroom. He pushed open the door, and I saw a huge whirlpool spa tub.

"I've been dying to have sex in this since the day I moved in. Want to try it out with me?"

"Sure," I said, whipping off my clothes.

"You're always so compliant," he joked, swiping my bouncing cock with his tongue.

I watched him turn up the taps, the water mixing beautifully with whatever fragrant oils he'd poured in. The water foamed slightly, the heady scent of tropical flowers driving me crazy as we kissed. He undressed and turned off the taps.

Naked and hard. Yep. Definitely our favorite state.

He took my hand after checking the water temperature. Totally adorable in my book. I stepped into the filmy liquid. There is something about hot water and a man's cock. The two are an item for sure. My cock got harder as I slid into the tub, leaning against the slick, warm walls. Dane turned on the whirlpool to a gentle mode then climbed in with me. He had some tricks up his sleeve I could tell.

"What are you up to?" I asked as he kissed me then began

to suck my cock.

He came off me for a moment. "You'll see." He grinned, then went right back to work. As he tongued and licked my balls and cock, I wanted to be in him, but he wanted me to experience a different kind of pleasure first.

Dane lifted my ass with both hands. It was easy in water. Suddenly, I felt a jet of very hot water aiming out of the spot beneath my ass and straight up my hole.

Oh my God!

The pleasure was immediate and intense. I couldn't believe how incredible it felt, especially with my cock imbedded in his hungry mouth. He sucked and pulled on me, and I came so hard I saw stars and planets, even that new unnamed one, and the sensation was unbelievable.

Of course, I reciprocated but by the time he was ready to shoot he wanted me to sit on that jet stream as he straddled me and rode my cock.

I was happy to fuck him any way he wanted, and with the water keeping him buoyant, I was happy to suck and fuck him at the same time as that hot water shot right into me. I tried hard not to come too soon but Dane's ass was so tight and juicy, I went berserk. We came together, Dane's cock erupting in my mouth.

"Isn't this a cool toy?" he asked as I held him to my hips. I was still coming, my pleasure immense and all for him. "Are you lost for words, Matty?"

I nodded, his cock bouncing against my wet lips. "Yeah." I turned off the taps and carried him to bed. We had some serious fucking to do.

Over the next few weeks, Dane and I saw a lot of each other. I'd FedExed the balance of his father's retainer to Christopher and his set of Dane's house keys, but apart from a text acknowledging that he'd received them, he stayed silent.

Ronin stayed with Dane.

And he didn't spray once. Not *once.*

They were joined at the foot. Dane's that is. Ronin loved Dane, and I was certain I'd lose an eye if I tried to pick up the cat and take him back home with me.

Dane introduced me to his two best friends, a lesbian couple with a seven-year-old son. I adored the kid. He was doing a class assignment on what he'd prefer if he had to be on a deserted island. Given the choice of being alone or with the one person he hated most in the world, he said, "I'd like to be with someone, so I would have something to eat."

We laughed every time we talked about that amazing kid.

Dane and I had so much fun together it was hard to delve back into my sordid business. I gave up my office because of the break-in and because I couldn't justify the expense. I picked up some routine cheating spouse work and operated out of my apartment. I'd decided to let Angus live there, and the nights I didn't sleep with Dane, I spent on my sofa. Angus and I arranged to split the rent, and we were both happy.

Dane occasionally asked about my work but seemed more intent on his own career. I happily let him focus on it. I wanted him to feel happy to be alive. I tried to create as little stress for him as possible. It wasn't hard turning around questions about my day to ask about his. Especially when it became apparent he was in line to direct a low-budget movie. I'm ashamed to admit that like almost everybody else in Hollywood, I'm a frustrated writer. I was fascinated by the scripts Dane gave me to read. They were truly horrible, but I knew that in this town a decent screenplay was not a prerequisite for a movie deal.

When Dane picked up three design gigs, including the job for Annie's agent, we celebrated with dinner at the most romantic place I knew, Inn of the Sixth Ray in Topanga Canyon. What I will always cherish is the smile on his face all night as we grazed on great food under a canopy of night stars and fairy lights in the trees. Then we ran home to fuck like bunnies.

He was still planning to open his art café, but apparently, he'd been having serious discussions with Thomas, the former gay porn star, who'd recovered from his brush with fate.

Thomas had been making money producing low-budget vampire movies that made big bucks according to him, and now Dane was going to direct his first mainstream feature for Thomas's company.

"It's all going to be shot locally," Dane told me when we had dinner one night at our favorite Thai place on Melrose. "Matt, I can't believe how lucky I am. My whole life changed. I met you, and it's all going right. Suddenly. Finally."

"I have something to tell you," I blurted. "I've been meaning to tell you for weeks. I'm sorry. I'm so sorry, but it's bugging me. I just don't want to lose you."

"What is it?"

"I'm a private detective. Your father hired me to find you. I cared about you as soon as I met you. I didn't mean to fall in love with you, but I did. And I do." I frowned, getting confused in my jumble of words. "I do. Love you."

He stared at me. "Is this a joke?"

I shook my head.

"You . . ." He put down his chopsticks, tilting his head to one side, narrowing his eyes at me. He stared off into space for a moment, then asked, "How did you find me?"

I told him everything.

And whoever said honesty is the best policy, especially in a relationship, was a lying asshole.

"I hate you," he said, dropping some money onto his plate. "I'm going home. Alone." He held up a hand. "And don't say another word. I'm so damned mad at you."

"What about—"

"No. Not another word." I was going to ask about the cat, but Dane stormed out, and I finished my meal. I was used to eating whilst upset. It was a way of life for me.

Outside the restaurant, clouds gathered, and I smelled rain on the horizon. We'd driven here in Dane's car, so I walked home. It was a long fucking walk, but I knew a couple who once a year walked from one end of Wilshire Boulevard to the other. Each and every year. It takes a lot of love to spend that much time with someone. And I'd hoped to do that with Dane.

I could walk to Santa Monica. Alone. Yeah. I could do it. I shuffled down Melrose feeling really sorry for myself. I kept noticing places that used to be other things. Soap Plant, a wacky store with wild gifts, was now a nail salon. The Last Woundup, a toy store specializing in wind-up toys . . . gone.

The Melting Pot, a fabulous restaurant in the eighties. Long gone. Bono's, Sonny Bono's American-Italian eatery, was gone. So was Sonny. He'd been a great host. I thought about Dane opening his art café. He'd be a great, convivial host, too.

The Bodhi Tree, my favorite bookstore in the whole world, was gone but the pretentious Urth Café next door was still there, so I snagged an outside table and ordered espresso.

I thought about Dane and how happy we'd been the last few weeks. It had been great. The thing about living in Los Angeles is that there are so few people who were here back in the day. So few understood its real culture. I knew it, I held onto it. Dane did too. I sipped my coffee and got on with my walk.

108

It was three A.M. when I got home and unlocked my door. I could smell Annie's faint perfume. The bedroom door was closed. I checked my cell phone for messages, and it hadn't been my imagination each time I'd checked before. There was no word from Dane.

I typed the words *I'd been wanting to say for weeks* into a text that I didn't send. I wrote, *Tu eres mi vida entera!* You are my whole world. One man had said it to another in our new favorite gay movie. It was too soon, or was it too late for me to say those words to him? I took a gamble because I knew I had to. I hit send. And then I lay back, wondering if my mom had ever made her court date.

The dark grey sky matched my mood the next morning as I met with a client at his offices over in Century City at nine o'clock. He was an Australian businessman, and I'd worked with him before. I disliked him intensely, but if liking a man was my criteria for taking on a client, I'd never have business.

He had a very cool setup in his ultra luxurious space on Avenue of the Stars. He had office suites and a private living area that I'd never seen. Not that I wanted to, but I did envy his plush digs.

John Randall was one of the least attractive men I'd ever seen. He had the face of a bulldog and a florid complexion that always made me think he was on the verge of a stroke. He was built like a tank and thought his expensive Brooks Brothers suits gave him some class. They did not.

But none of this was what bothered me. What bothered me was that he was a married man with many children and an outspoken critic of gay people, black people, single mothers, single fathers, Jews, Asians . . . anyone who didn't embody his high standards.

And yet, he had numerous mistresses and whores scattered across the U.S. He'd thought that sowing his oats in a different country would absolve him of responsibility, but for all his business acumen he seemed quite stupid. He'd tried to tell me he didn't think he'd have to pay child support because it was nonexistent in Australia.

I'd had to point out that America is a litigious society and child support was mandatory. He'd been horrified when he had trouble arriving at LAX on one occasion because his passport had been flagged under a new law designed to catch deadbeat dads.

He'd brought me in on three different cases of women suing him for child support. I'd helped stamp out all three fires by negotiating with the woman personally, thereby making all those involved very happy.

"I have a new problem," he said the moment his secretary had brought us coffee in his private conference room and left us alone. I stole one last admiring glance of his spectacular view of Century City's elegant buildings and grabbed my cup. I filled it quickly. There had been, as usual, nothing by way of food in my apartment when I'd awoken this morning and, from memory, Randall's coffee was always good.

*Not as good as Dane's*, a small, lost voice whispered inside my brain.

"What's the problem?" I asked.

"I've apparently fathered another child."

Arching a brow in his direction, I said, "I take it congratulations aren't in order?"

He gave an ironic shake of the head. "Not likely. And this one's tough."

Why? I wondered.

"This one happened sixteen years ago." For once, John Randall seemed dismayed. "The irony is, I loved this woman. Genuinely loved her. I almost left my wife for her, but she wouldn't let me." His voice broke. I stared at him. I'd never seen genuine emotion pouring out of him before. "She said I had children at home and they needed me."

He fell silent. He got up and walked around the room. He touched the mounted Aboriginal art, one of the first cases he'd brought me in on. Somebody had stolen his treasures, which had been taken out of the country illegally in the first place. But that was another story . . .

"I always regretted letting Donna break up with me. I've always loved her and isn't it ironic? She is probably the only woman apart from my wife who truly loves me. And she's never asked me for a thing."

For a moment I thought he might bawl.

"She was and is the most beautiful woman I've ever met," he said. For the first time since I'd worked for him, I watched him gazing out of his window as if he finally realized what a magnificent view he had. "She was the one that got away."

He turned to me. "You ever been in love with someone like that?" Before he could respond, he said, "I let her leave because she was right to be angry with me. I'd lied to her. Told her I was a single man. Sixteen years ago, the world wasn't what it is now. She could have checked on me via the Internet. When I told her the truth, she didn't want me anymore.

"Maybe if I'd tried a little harder . . . maybe if I'd pushed, I wouldn't have lost all those years, and I'd have gotten to know my little girl."

"You just found out you have a daughter with . . . Donna?"

He nodded and let out a profound sigh. Though red-rimmed, his eyes didn't shed a tear. I knew he was worried now and I hadn't realized it when I'd first walked in.

"What's happened?" I asked, his anxiety reaching me.

"Donna called me last night. Her daughter . . . our daughter has vanished. She thinks she's alive because she's been using the ATM card Donna gave her, and there are text messages on her cell phone. Donna checked. God!" He thumped the table. "If I lose that child before I even get a chance to know her . . ."

He didn't finish his sentence. He put his hand into his suit pocket and produced a photograph. I almost fell off my chair.

"She's sixteen?" I asked. I couldn't believe it.

"Yes. And apparently quite precocious."

That was one way of putting it. I stared at the photo of the young woman I knew as Annie and shook my head.

"What's her name?" I asked, my voice low.

"Annie." John sat down, taking the photo and staring at it. "She named her after my mother."

I could have taken John for a financial ride and dazzled him with my investigative skills, but I couldn't. A lost child, a lost love . . . No. Those cases sucked the big one.

"This is your lucky day, Mr. Randall."

"Yeah? Why?"

"I know her. I know exactly where she is."

He stared at me. "Are you psychic?"

"No. She's in my apartment. She's my brother's girlfriend."

I called Angus over John Randall's protestations that he wanted the police involved.

"She's sixteen," he kept repeating as if I were a dolt and hadn't understood the first time. I got Angus on the first ring and asked him to bring Annie to the Century City office.

"What's going on?" he asked.

"She's sixteen."

"She's . . . *what?*"

"And she's a runaway. Her father wants to see her."

"She doesn't have a father."

"Yes, Angus. She does. I'm sitting here with him now."

I had to convince my brother to bring her here. He called me three times on the way, petrified that Annie's father would have him arrested.

"I'm here," I promised him. "I won't let anyone hurt you." It took some doing not to let John Randall call Donna. I was pretty sure she'd arrive with an arsenal of law enforcement, but I wanted father and daughter to have a moment together.

I also wanted him to see that Angus wasn't some pedophile but a computer geek who loved Annie.

It was difficult, but I also had to point out that Donna had lied to both him and Annie for sixteen years. When that broken girl arrived and fell into her father's arms, I felt I'd handled things the right way.

"You look just like your mother," he kept saying. He was a lot nicer to my brother once he realized he'd had no idea Annie was just sixteen.

"How old are you?" John asked, a sharp glint to the eye.

"Nineteen, sir."

"Thank God you're not like that moronic fifty-year-old actor who married that teenager."

He called Donna, and the five of us spent some awkward but mostly quality time together. And John was right. Mother and daughter were both gorgeous. Annie agreed to move back home.

Poor Angus. Once again, he'd have to live without love.

"You can date her," John said, making Donna bristle. "But she's staying home with us."

"Us?" Donna asked.

"Us." John gave her a look that would have smelted metal.

"Thank you, sir," Angus said, and I tugged his sleeve, dragging him out of the office. In the elevator back to the parking garage, we looked at each other.

"Are we marked for life or something?" Angus asked.

"No. Why?"

"How come our lives are so seriously fucked up?"

His cell phone rang as we got to his vehicle. He grinned. "They've invited me to lunch."

"See. Not so fucked up." I gave him a hug and watched him sprint back to the elevators.

That was one of us happy. I thought a lot about the notion as I angled out of the building and paid the thirty dollar parking fee. Damned Century City. Orson Welles once said that human beings thought they had a right to be happy, but he insisted they weren't entitled to it. It had to be earned.

He was so right. And I knew something else. Love, real love wasn't for sale, but its value was fathomless. The price of losing it . . . inestimable.

I drove all the way to Baldwin Hills in search of the man I didn't want to be without. I didn't have my words sorted, but I was willing to do whatever he wanted to prove that I wanted to love him, that I wanted to be with him.

I found him at home, though getting him to open the door was the least of my worries. Getting him to listen to me was a whole 'nother thing.

"I'm not ready to speak to you," he said.

"Then can I kiss you?"

"What?"

"I want to kiss you. I need to kiss you. My whole mouth misses kissing you."

"Have you been drinking?"

"No."

"Can't you give me some space?"

"No. I can't."

"I'm mad at you."

"So you said. You can't kiss when you're mad?"

He looked at me, and I felt something furry at my feet. Ronin.

"Traitor," Dane said when the cat flopped on my feet. Dane was dressed in pajama bottoms. My pajama bottoms.

"Can I come in?" I asked.

"I guess." He let me in. The place felt sad. As sad as we both were.

"My dad told me last night that you wanted to tell me yourself that he hired you. You want coffee? I bet there was none at home."

"You guessed right. Everything I love is here."

He didn't say anything for a moment, busying himself with making espresso.

"I suppose I should be happy that they love me so much. He also said you returned most of the money he gave you, so I have to give you some props. I'd say you're basically an honest person."

"Yes, I am."

"But I don't know . . . a private investigator. I should have figured it out. I Googled you and found one Matt Killian. A cop who was shot and became a PI. I didn't think you were the same Matt Killian. Your life story is like a movie."

"Yeah. A horror movie."

He laughed then. That fantastic laugh that always made me happy. And hard.

"Damn you," he said when I took him in my arms and kissed him. His cock betrayed him as it got hard and responded to my touch.

"I don't want you," he said, even as I got him to the floor and ripped my pajama bottoms off his beautiful body. "I love you," he said as I kissed him. "But I don't want you."

"Uh-huh." My mouth moved over every inch of his face and body. I got to his cock and licked it.

"I love you, too," I said.

"Tell me that when you're inside me," he muttered. "Hurry up and fuck me."

"Don't worry," I said. "I will."

The cat brushed past us both. Outside, I could hear the rain start to pour, and the coffee started to heat up, smelling amazing.

Beneath my still-clothed body, the man I loved tore at my shirt buttons and reached for my mouth with his. He whispered against my lips the very words I said over and over to him all the time in my mind.

*"Tu eres mi vida entera."*

You are my whole world.

# About the Author

A.J. Llewellyn lives in California, but dreams of living in Hawaii. Frequent trips to all the islands, bags of Kona coffee in her fridge and a healthy collection of Hawaiian records keep this writer refueled. A.J. loves male/male erotica, has a passion for all animals—especially the dog, the cat and the turtle. A.J. believes that love is a song best sung out loud.

To find out more about A. J., visit www.ajllewellyn.com or you can email her at AJ@AJLlewellyn.com.

www.ingramcontent.com/pod-product-compliance
Lightning Source LLC
Chambersburg PA
CBHW060642130626
46555CB00002B/914